LIVING THE DREAM

M J HARDY

LIVING THE DREAM

Can you really trust your friends or are they keeping secrets that will destroy you?

Four women who are living the dream.
Fast cars
Beautiful Homes
Fantastic holidays
Gorgeous Husbands and lots of shopping.

Perfection comes at a price and it's payback time. Four lives intertwined and heading for a fall.
When you're living the dream sometimes you wake up and find reality is a nightmare.
Beware the Ten Commandments because you break them at your peril.

Suspenseful and shocking and one hell of a ride. Who will be the last woman standing and who will she have to step on to get there?

PROLOGUE

THE DAY IT BEGAN
Arabella

*M*iranda heads towards us, looking a little pale. Venetia rolls her eyes as Fleur pipes up, "Well, how was it? What did she say?"

Miranda sits in the leather seat opposite and shrugs. "Oh, you know, the usual."

We stare at her expectantly, and I don't miss the slight tremble to her bottom lip and the expression of blind panic in her eyes. However, she soon pulls the mask back in place and says brightly, "Bloody charlatan. I'm convinced she says the same thing to everyone. Why don't we compare notes at the end?"

Fleur grins. "I'll go next. I can always spot a fake."

I watch her head purposefully towards the door and stare with surprise as Miranda reaches for a glass of water with a slight shake of her hand. Venetia catches my eye, and it's obvious she's noticed it too and not for the first time I wonder if this was such a good idea.

Fleur organised it as a bit of a laugh, and I suppose we all thought it would be. Mind you, I've always been a little scared of dabbling in things like this and, apparently, I was right to be concerned.

We make polite conversation for twenty minutes before the door opens and Fleur exits the room. For once she appears to have lost a little of her bravado and swagger and looks well – shaken.

She catches my eye and laughs nervously. "Total nonsense. It's all quite laughable, really."

Venetia looks worried. "Maybe I should give it a miss. I mean, I don't want to waste money on an imposter."

Fleur fixes her with a hard stare and says roughly, "Rubbish. You go next and don't even try to back out. We're all in this together and nobody gets to dodge anything."

She fixes Venetia with a hard glare, and so, with a sigh, Venetia stands and says somewhat belligerently, "Ok, but for the record, I'm doing this under duress."

Fleur sighs as Venetia disappears through the door at the end and peers across at Miranda. "Are you ok, babe?"

"Nothing a bottle of wine won't cure." She laughs, but her usual confidence has diminished and I wonder what on earth Desdemona Fortune is saying in there?

When Fleur told us about the fortune teller, we were all sceptical. I've never believed in anything not based on fact, but Fleur told us a friend of hers recommended her and that Desdemona was spot on. She organised the visit for us all as a bit of a laugh, a girly day out that will end with an alcoholic lunch at our favourite bistro nearby. We envisaged laughing about the premonitions and sharing tales of coincidence and amazing predictions. However, from the expressions on their faces, it was far from the laugh they thought it would be.

For once, the conversation is minimal. Instead, my two friends seem fixated on anything other than making eye contact or actual conversation. Fleur flicks through a fashion magazine, but it's obvious she's not reading it. Miranda is checking her phone, but the screen has remained the same the entire time and she's pre-occupied with whatever it is she heard and I shiver as I wait nervously for my turn.

We glance up as the door opens and Venetia heads towards us, looking angry and I stare at her in surprise as she says roughly, "Hurry up, Arabella, the sooner you get your turn over with, the sooner we leave. I can't wait to get out of this place. It's bloody creepy."

I head towards the door at the end and falter a little. From the reactions of my three friends, it's doubtful I'm going to like what's behind it and so I try to keep an open mind and knock nervously before heading inside.

* * *

The light in the room is dark and mysterious, and I peer around with trepidation. Velvet walls add to the sense of mystery and anticipation and the only light in the room is from the glow of many candles set around the perimeter.

My heart starts banging and my mouth is dry and I run my tongue around my lips nervously as I make out the figure sitting at the table in the centre.

The woman waiting is a textbook fortune teller. Her head is covered by a silk scarf and the gold hoops in her ears reinforce the image. Her face is calm, and she projects an air of serenity as she smiles mysteriously and gestures to the seat in front of her.

As I take the seat offered, she holds out her hand and says in a soft voice, "Cross my hand with silver and you shall learn the future."

I grip hold of the shiny fifty pence piece that we were instructed to bring and lay it on her outstretched palm, wishing that was all it cost because, if I remember rightly, it was ten times that when I paid online to book my appointment.

The business side of this settles my heart a little as I try to tell myself that's all this is—business. Desdemona makes a living from theatrics and we are pandering to that by joining the gullible idiots who pass through these doors each day.

I dig deep inside for courage and face Desdemona Fortune with cynicism and disbelief and steel myself for what she's about to reveal.

I stare as she rolls the coin around her fingers before raising it to her lips. She kisses it and then places it in a money box by the side and smiles. "Thank you."

She reaches out and takes my hands in hers and I stare down at the tanned, wrinkled fingers that are gripping my own so tightly and try to relax.

For a minute, she merely holds me and closes her eyes, appearing to be in a trance.

My heart beats frantically because the whole situation is one of theatrics and effects and despite my scepticism, even I'm apparently a believer.

It surprises me when her hands start to shake a little, and I experience the vibrations through my fingers and glance at her in surprise. Her eyes remain closed, but I register a pulse twitching at her temple and her breathing becomes hard and laboured. It's strange watching her go through some kind of spasm and I tell myself it's just part of her act. It almost becomes embarrassing because she says nothing as she holds onto my hands with an iron grip and my sweat joins hers as she grips me tightly.

Then, when I'm totally spooked, she opens her eyes and the expression on her face drives fear to my heart. Her eyes are filled with tears and so much pain I wonder if she's about to have a heart attack. She shakes her head frantically and gasps and moans like a grieving widow, "Nooo…"

She grips me tighter and I stare in shock as the tears bubble up and spill over her cheeks as she rasps, "It's too much. I can't deal with it."

I fidget in my seat and say nervously, "Is everything ok?"

She shakes her head and her lip trembles as she chokes out, "Beware the Ten Commandments."

Now I'm uncomfortable and whisper, "What do you mean?"

Turning away, she reaches for a handkerchief and says roughly, "Terrible things. Your future is shrouded in grief and shadows. Nothing was clear except for total devastation. You're not safe and your life is…"

I'm alarmed and say slightly hysterically, "What did you see?"

She leans back in her seat and visibly shakes as she stares at me with so much pity I find it difficult to breathe.

"Beware the Ten Commandments."

I feel the anger bubbling inside me and wonder if this is what made Venetia so angry. My friends are right. She has probably said the same thing to all of us, so I take it all with a pinch of salt and say briskly, "Ok, what exactly do you mean by that? I mean, I thought you may tell me I was due to start a family, or go on a nice holiday. You know the type of thing."

To be honest, as I voice the words I had hoped to hear, I realise why I agreed to come in the first place. To say I'm desperate for a child is an understatement, and I hoped she was going to tell me one is in my immediate future.

She checks herself and leans forward, whispering. "Take care of yourself, Arabella, because no one else will."

The knot that's forming inside me is growing by the second. What does she mean? Of course, Anthony will take care of me. He's my husband and we're mad about one another.

I wish I'd never come and say firmly, "Is that it? What did you see exactly? I mean, if it's so bad, why can't you tell me what it is and I'll prepare for it? It's easy to say words that aren't backed up by fact, but you've got to give me something more to go on."

She appears worried and nods, before her eyes fall to the door behind me.

"The other women, they may be your friends, but they hold the key to your future. Stay guarded and believe nothing. You need to be strong for what fate has in store for you, and the only one you've really got is yourself."

"Why? What's going to happen?"

She slumps back in her seat and closes her eyes, saying in a small voice, "A nightmare."

I stare in confusion as she stands and heads towards a door at the back of the room. With one hand on the handle and still with her back to me, she says in a defeated voice, "Leave–all of you! The energy you have brought into my space is bad. I don't want you here—go!"

Before I can say anything, she heads through the door, slamming it behind her, leaving me feeling like a fool. An angry fool at that and I take the anger bubbling up under the surface with me as I make my way to the opposite door.

Miranda was right — bloody charlatan.

* * *

Lunch is a totally different affair than the one we envisaged. As we all sit gloomily nursing large glasses of wine, I wonder who will be the first one to voice what just happened.

It turns out to be Venetia because she sighs and sets her glass down, saying wearily, "Ok, I'll go first. That woman, well, she speaks in riddles. I'm not sure what I thought she'd say, but tell me something at least. All she told me was my future was dark and there was no hope."

She laughs nervously. "What's that supposed to mean? I tried to ask her and she fixed me with a hate-filled look and told me to beware the Ten Commandments."

Fleur interrupts. "She said that to me, too. I asked if Anton was going to get his transfer deal and she stared at me as if I were an idiot. She shook her head and said exactly the same. Beware the Ten Commandments."

Miranda nods. "Same. It was creepy. She kept staring at me and shaking her head. I asked her what she saw, and she almost spat the words at me. Those same bloody words she said to you about the Ten Commandments. To be honest, I don't know what to make of it all. I'm inclined to demand a refund because she has told me absolutely nothing."

They stare at me and I nod in agreement. "Same. Beware the Ten Commandments. What do you think she meant by that?"

Fleur shrugs. "From what I remember, it's all that stuff about not stealing or committing adultery. To be honest, she must be mad, because why would any of us steal? We have more money between us than most banks and as for adultery, well, does she even realise who my husband is?"

As usual, she looks around at us smugly as Miranda says somewhat cattily, "Since when was Anton your husband?"

I notice the colour rise in Fleur's cheeks as she snaps irritably, "A minor detail. He will be soon; once he gets the season out of the way and if I know him, he's planning a beachside wedding in a tropical paradise as a lovely surprise."

I catch Venetia's eye and she shakes her head. Fleur is desperate to make the step up from a footballer's girlfriend to an official wife. Anton doesn't seem in any hurry though, despite what my friend just said. He appears more than happy with things the way they are and, despite the constant nagging of his girlfriend, has yet to make it official.

We don't hang around and soon return home to the cul-de-sac of four homes that make up The Chase. An executive group of homes that sit behind security gates in the leafy suburb of Esher. As we all make our way to our respective homes, I wonder if things will change as a result of our afternoon.

As it happens — everything changes.

PART I

ARABELLA

CHAPTER 1

ARABELLA

$\mathcal{T}$he door slams and my heart lifts.

He's home.

Dropping my oven gloves, I head into the large, marble tiled hallway to greet my husband. He flings his keys on the hall table and opens his arms as I jump into them. As they fold around me, I cling to the man I love as if I haven't seen him in months instead of the usual working day.

As I snuggle against him, he strokes my hair, whispering, "I missed you, Bella."

I stroke his face and whisper, "Me too."

He lowers his lips to mine and we share a deep kiss that comes with the sort of love that unites souls. He is my soul mate, my love and my husband. The man I promised to love forever, through sickness and in health, and I meant every word.

He pulls back and grins, "So, how was your day, darling? I hope it was a lot better than mine."

I glance at him with concern as he shakes his head. "Don't mind me, it's just the usual problems that go with being a successful film producer. You know the type of things, actors forgetting their lines, stunts going wrong and catering not turning up."

I throw him a sympathetic look and he sighs. "I need a drink more than anything right now."

"Of course, come through and I'll fix it while you tell me what went wrong."

He follows me into possibly the largest domestic kitchen ever built. It was the wow factor of the house we chose together and is the heartbeat of our home. Warm, welcoming and yet sleek and modern, consisting of chrome, steel and granite, designed by the best kitchen company in the country. It cost more than some people spend on a house and yet to us it was nothing. Money has never been tight and what we want — we get. I suppose it's one of the benefits of being married to a man who has delivered more award-winning programmes than any other and is in demand all over the world. However, to me, he's my husband; the man I love and my best friend.

As I pour him his usual gin and tonic with lots of ice and lemon, he kicks off his shoes and leans against the counter. "Thanks, darling, coming home to you makes sense of it all. If it wasn't for you, I'd be a screwed-up mess and probably festering in an alley somewhere."

I roll my eyes as I pour myself a glass and say lightly, "Idiot. You can pretend that things are difficult, but I know you too well. You enjoy a myriad of assistants to do your bidding, and the only difficult decision you make is whether to take one hour for lunch or two. You're a fraud and you know it?"

He raises his glass to mine. "Busted by my own wife. I should have known better."

I busy myself preparing dinner while he heads off to shower and change and as I work, I feel that smug sense of satisfaction when I think about how great my life is. A handsome husband, an amazing home and money that never dries up. I am part of a group of friends who complete my dream life and I wouldn't change a thing. Well, perhaps just one. I want a family so badly it hurts, but Anthony is so busy he keeps on telling me we should put it off. He wants to be home for his children, not working every hour, and says it's unfair to bring children into our fast-paced life.

I actually disagree because it hurts me so much when I see mothers with children in town and on the television. It always reinforces the fact that something big is missing from my life that all the money in the world can't replace.

Sighing, I turn my attention to dishing up our supper and admonish myself for being so selfish. Anthony's right, it isn't the right time and I should know that more than most. My own parents had just one child—me and then spent the rest of my life passing me on to anyone who would take me. Nannies, boarding school, finishing school and university. Even my holidays were spent bettering myself by sending me off to work in poor countries and internships to grow my CV. I had everything as a child except actual parents who loved me. They are now strangers because they never wanted me to be part of their lives and that, as it turns out, is fine by me. I may have never loved them. It certainly feels that way, so why would I want that for my children? No, Anthony is right, now is not the time—the trouble is, when will be?

Over dinner, I tell him about the visit to the fortune teller and he raises his eyes. "Typical Fleur. I'm surprised at you though, darling. I wouldn't have thought it was your thing."

I shrug, "It isn't, but where it concerns Fleur, it's best to go along with what she arranges."

He shakes his head. "You never used to be a doormat. What happened?"

I stare at him in surprise and he winks to take the sting from his words.

13

"Doormat? I'm hardly that."

He shrugs, which irritates me even more. "How does pleasing my friends make me a doormat?"

Helping himself to more salad, he smiles. "Nothing; it's what I like most about you. You're loyal, funny and kind. It's what makes you so popular, but I just wish you would stand up for yourself occasionally. Take today, for instance. If you didn't want to go, you should have said no, but you went anyway. Instead, you followed Fleur to a place that brought you no joy whatsoever, and I'm guessing you paid a lot of money for the privilege. Just harden up a little darling, that's all I'm saying."

I groan. "That's easy for you to say. You don't have to actually face the woman."

Anthony laughs and reaching across, grabs my hand and squeezes it gently. "To be honest, I don't understand what Anton sees in her. Even I can see she's a gold digger."

I stare at him in shock as he shrugs. "She is, which is why he probably hasn't made it official. I'm guessing he makes use of the benefits she brings and turns a blind eye to her flaws. You mark my words, though; the shine will soon wear off and the excitement fades. That little lady's days are numbered because I'm pretty sure Anton has an endless stream of wannabes lining up to take her place. Just be careful; that's all I'm saying."

He carries on eating and despite his harsh words, I agree with him. Fleur and Anton haven't been together long and even though she's drop-dead gorgeous with a body to die for, she has a devious mind and a hard exterior. Perhaps Anthony's right and I should distance myself because I don't want to be caught in the explosion when that particular bubble bursts.

CHAPTER 2

"*R*emind me again why we're doing this?"

I groan and glance over at Miranda, who looks as if she's about to keel over.

Grinning, I nod towards the perfect specimen of a man that's putting us through our paces. "I expect it has a lot to do with the view."

We giggle and gaze across at the only reason we came. Darren. Our total Adonis personal trainer and the man who runs the boot camp in the grounds of the country club we all religiously head to every week for fitness, socialising and more eye candy than a woman can stand.

Miranda giggles. "I've got to hand it to Fleur. She was spot on with this. If it wasn't for Darren, I'd be wrapped up warm in my bed and dreaming of a man like him beside me."

"Keep up ladies, you're wasting valuable energy by talking."

Trying not to laugh, we set about doing what Darren says and try desperately to remember why we're here.

Despite the ungodly hour of 6.30am, we flock here in droves twice a week just to lust after the total God that runs this class. Spaces are limited, and it requires setting an alarm the moment the slots are released each week just to grab one of them. Luckily for us, we have all managed it this week and, as I catch sight of Fleur, I try not to laugh.

Venetia catches me and rolls her eyes, and I can see why. Unlike the rest of us, Fleur turns up here in full make-up with her hair neatly scraped back into her sleek ponytail, wearing designer fitness gear that costs a small fortune. Her manicured nails look as if they never see housework and she spends the entire class trying to prove she is better than the rest of us at just about everything. She always positions herself as close to Darren as possible and I'm sure it's so he gets a clear view of her cleavage as she squats in front of him.

I must look a hot mess with the sweat dripping down my back that creates alarming damp patches all over my vest to match the ones down below, because Darren is seriously hot. The country club wasn't silly in signing him up because without him as the main attraction, it's doubtful anyone would bother to come.

I watch Venetia going at it like she does everything in life. Totally committed and with a seriousness that got her where she is today. Out of all of us, she's the only one with a full-time job and isn't here much. She's an Air Stewardess so is away a lot which can't be easy on her husband Matthew, who is left behind running the Airline that she works for.

"And breathe…"

I watch Darren smouldering across from me and my heart flutters - again.

"Great work, girls. I'll see you all on Wednesday and remember to drink some water after that workout."

He turns away and I watch with amusement as Fleur grabs hold of his arm and pulls him close, whispering something in his ear. Her body language couldn't be more suggestive if she tried as she rests her ample chest on his arm and flirts like a pro, demanding his attention as only she can.

Venetia stands next to me, drinking deeply from her water bottle, and says irritably, "Look at her, what a tease. You know, I can see why wags get such a bad press. Just look at her. She couldn't be more stereotypical if she tried."

Miranda nods. "She doesn't help herself, that's for sure."

Fleur's soft giggle carries across the grass towards us and Miranda scowls. "It's not fair. Why is life so cruel? I mean, look at her, she has everything. Stunning looks, amazing body and the fittest guy out of all of them, and it's still not enough. To be honest, sometimes I really hate Fleur."

I stare at her in surprise. "You don't mean that."

Miranda scowls. "I bloody well do. To be honest, she is seriously grating on me lately. We're expected to do everything she says and if one of us has a suggestion she doesn't like; she puts her foot down. Take that stupid fortune teller as an example. None of us wanted to go and yet she made it so we couldn't refuse. I don't know about the rest of you, but I've had enough."

Venetia nods in agreement. "You're right. Maybe we should all stand firm and put her in her place. I mean, after all, she's only here because her boyfriend's successful."

Miranda nods and I feel uncomfortable speaking about Fleur like this. For all her faults, she does have a kind heart and if she didn't organise things, none of us would have half the fun that we do.

Luckily, the conversation stops as she heads towards us, looking extremely pleased with herself.

"Weep in your beds ladies, because I've just secured myself the hottest personal trainer in history. Darren has agreed to do a little one on one with me on Friday lunchtimes. I'm not going to lie; I feel quite smug about this."

Miranda appears envious as Venetia snorts, "And what's

Anton going to say about that? I'm pretty sure he won't be comfortable with his, um... girlfriend, getting close and personal with another man on his hard-earned money."

Miranda nods. "Yes, maybe you should ask him first."

Fleur snaps, "Anton wants me to be as fit as possible, and after all, he gets to reap the rewards. You know, Venetia, you're just jealous because your husband is nowhere near as fit as mine and you must work for a living."

We look at her in stunned silence as Venetia says icily, "For your information, I work because I want to. Matthew has begged me to give up work so we can start a family and I've dug my heels in because I don't want to be a kept woman, unlike some around here."

She glares around at us all and storms towards the changing room as Fleur shakes her head. "Ooh, I touched a nerve there. I'm guessing it's a different story than the one she's telling us. I mean, Anton told me that Matthew loves the fact she still works because he can't stand breathing the same air as her."

She looks at her Rolex and says in a light voice, "Well, I can't stand here gossiping all day. I must shower and change and head to the spa for my sports massage. Catch you later, ladies."

As we watch her go, Miranda shakes her head. "That was intense. I don't know about you, Arabella, but I felt quite uncomfortable there for a moment. Why do women have to be so bitchy? I mean, we're all friends and should have each other's backs, don't you think?"

Nodding, I grab my water bottle and start walking with her back to the changing rooms. "I agree. Have you noticed these bitchy comments seem to be coming more often lately? Do you think there's some sort of issue between the two of them?"

"Maybe, but I expect it's because they're just different

people. I mean, Venetia is quite abrupt with everyone and doesn't suffer fools gladly. I'm a little envious of her, though."

I glance at her in surprise. "Why?"

Suddenly, my friend looks so sad it takes my breath away as she says in a small voice, "At least Matthew wants to spend time with her; I wish James felt the same about me."

Reaching out, I take her hand and say softly, "He loves you; everyone can see that. What makes you think otherwise?"

"I'm not sure, really. He works hard, I know that, but when he is home, he's so... well, distant actually. I've tried to draw him out of himself, but he's like a closed book these days and I wonder if something's wrong that he's not telling me about."

I'm not sure what to say and just look at her sympatheti-cally before she whispers, "Do you think he's having an affair?"

Her words shock me and I immediately shake my head. "Of course not, he adores you."

She shrugs. "I thought so too once."

She sighs and then switches the subject. "What about you? How are things with Anthony?"

Trying not to sound too smug, I say softly, "Great, actu-ally. He's like the rest of the men and works hard, but when he's home, we enjoy each other's company."

She smiles and I feel a pang as I say sadly, "Although Venetia's words made me a little envious too."

"Why?"

"Because if Anthony told me he wanted to start a family, I would be on it like a shot."

"Doesn't he want kids, then?"

Miranda says it with surprise and I shake my head. "One day, but not now. He told me he wanted to be there for his children and because he's working so hard, it wouldn't be fair."

Miranda nods, but even I can see she doesn't agree with his reasoning, which only amplifies the fact that I also don't share his view. I want children and don't want to wait a minute more, but the trouble is, Anthony doesn't agree, which leaves me wondering if this is something that will ultimately rip us apart.

CHAPTER 3

ARABELLA

"*M*ust we go tonight?"

I smile as Anthony's arms wrap around me and pull me close. He nuzzles my neck and kisses it softly before spinning me around to kiss me long and hard. I melt against him as I always do and wish for the umpteenth time that we could miss this dinner tonight, but know we can't.

I pull back and smile ruefully. "I'm sorry, darling, but we have to go. It's Fleur's birthday, and you know what that means?"

He groans. "A night spent watching her milk Anton for even more of his money while flaunting it at the rest of us."

I say crossly. "You sound just like Venetia. Goodness, she's got some bee in her bonnet about Fleur and it's increasingly hard to ignore the animosity she directs at her. To be honest, Fleur has been nothing but nice since she moved here and maybe she is a kept woman, but she genuinely loves Anton. It's obvious."

Anthony raises his eyes and I snap. "Stop it, you don't know her like I do. Give the poor girl a break and then perhaps you'll see what the rest of us do."

I turn away and pull on the diamond choker that Anthony bought me for our third wedding anniversary and try to ignore the warning sirens going off in my head. Tonight may prove to be difficult, and once the alcohol starts flowing, I'm guessing so will the pent-up emotions and recriminations that have been festering for weeks now.

We make our way the short distance to Fleur and Anton's house, which is a mirror image of the rest of the houses in The Chase, which consist of palatial executive homes surrounded by manicured lawns and herbaceous borders. The plants that grow here are crafted with precision with not a leaf out of place. Impressive driveways are illuminated by state-of-the-art lighting and the cars that sit on them cost more than most people earn in a lifetime. Privilege, wealth and decadence sit behind the electric gates of The Chase and reflect the personalities of its occupants. People who live charmed lives and have absolutely nothing to complain about but do their best to do so, anyway. Does wealth bring happiness? In our case, it would appear not.

As we walk, I try to think of one other couple here that doesn't have issues, us included, and a shiver passes through me as I worry once again about what the fortune teller said. Anthony puts a protective arm around my fur-lined shoulders and says sweetly, "Are you cold, darling?" He gives me a gentle squeeze and I sigh, "Are we ok, Anthony?"

He looks surprised. "Of course we are. Why do you say that?"

"I don't know. It's just this is all too good to be true. Something's got to give and I'm fearful for us sometimes."

He stops and puts his hands on my shoulders and looks me firmly in the eye. "I love you, Arabella, and that's all we need. Even if we lose our wealth, our home and the clothes off our back, that will never change. You are everything to me, and that makes us the richest couple I know."

He smiles and I register the love in his eyes and my heart settles. I'm not sure why, probably because it's never far from my mind I say hesitantly, "I want a baby."

He looks at me in shock and I can understand why. We are standing in the middle of The Chase on a starlit night talking about everything but children. My heart sinks at the expression in his eye and the tears well up in mine as he turns away abruptly and drops his hands from my shoulders. "We spoke about this, Arabella. Why now?"

"Because the need is overwhelming me, Anthony. It's becoming the only thing I can think about. I know what you said, but I can't stop this need inside me to be a mother. Other people manage to work and have children. We can too, I really believe that."

He heads towards Anton's house and says sharply, "I'm not discussing this now. You certainly choose your moments, darling, and this is typical of you."

I struggle to keep up with him and say roughly, "What do you mean, typical of me?"

He spins around and I'm surprised at the fire in his eyes as he snaps, "You never know when it's the right time and place. Throwing this out here in the street when we have no time to discuss it. For god's sake, Arabella, grow up."

He walks away, leaving me open-mouthed behind him.

I'm conscious of our neighbours leaving their house and glance up as Miranda and James head towards me. I say lightly, "Hey guys. You look lovely Miranda."

I don't miss the surprise on their faces as they notice Anthony standing waiting by Anton and Fleur's front door, and I roll my eyes. "Sorry, he's always impatient to get to places, and I got a stone in my shoe. Chivalry is sure dead around here."

They smile but I can tell they know exactly what this is, a difference of opinion leading to another domestic. Sighing, I walk with them to join my husband and wonder if we'll ever agree on this. Perhaps I shouldn't have said anything, and he's right, now is not the time, but it's becoming obvious this is a matter that won't wait. I want a baby and if Anthony won't give me one, perhaps I should find a man who will.

CHAPTER 4

ARABELLA

*W*alking into Fleur and Anton's home is like walking onto a film set. Their home is everything one would expect from the home of a highly paid footballing superstar. Chandeliers twinkle from the ceiling and cast their light over the mirrored furniture and deep piled scatter rugs sit on top of a shiny marble tiled floor. Huge mirrors reveal the unworthy looking back at them and amazing flower arrangements sit on top of streak-free surfaces. The air wafts with expensive scent and the soft music that pipes through the house creates a welcoming atmosphere.

The man of the house holds his partner's hand carefully as they smile their welcome. Anton Richardson is an impressive man. Toe-curling good looks complement a body that most men would die for. Muscles ripple under the silk shirt he wears, and the tattoos that look good on men like him decorate every inch of visible skin. His dark hair frames a face of masculine beauty and the sparkle in his eyes reduces women to pools of wanton thoughts and desire.

Fleur stands beside him looking as if she's just stepped

out of Vogue. Her golden hair is immaculately placed on top of her head, with just a well-placed curl hanging down on either side, framing her exquisite face. Sparkling blue eyes smile their welcome as her ruby painted lips turn upward in a smile. Her slim, svelte, figure, causes envy among women everywhere and the white silk pantsuit she wears, clings to her body like a glove, wrapping her curves in a silken embrace and causing men to drool over what can only be described as pure perfection.

I don't miss the amazing ruby that hangs down around her neck matching the earrings that sparkle in her earlobes. Yes, Anton and Fleur are a couple made in Heaven and should reside in a museum for perfection for the entire world to drool over.

Pushing aside my envy, I kiss both of them three times on the cheek and say happily, "Happy birthday, Fleur. You look beautiful."

She blushes prettily and gratefully accepts the ribbon bound package I thrust into her hand.

"Thank you, darling, it's so good of you to come."

Anthony smiles. "Thanks for inviting us."

They turn their attention to Miranda and James and then say warmly, "Come through. Venetia and Matthew are here already. Let us fix you some champagne, or something more spirited if you prefer."

We follow them into the huge living area filled with large settees covered with luxurious fur throws. A welcoming fire dances in the grate and complements the many candles that burn on every available surface.

I notice Anthony head over to greet Venetia and Matthew and follow him, registering the strained expression in Venetia's eye as we approach. Anthony kisses her on the cheek and Matthew smiles and does the same to me. "Hey, Arabella. You look lovely."

Glancing down at the red silk dress I bought from Harvey Nichols, I smile my thanks. "How are things with you, Matthew?"

He smiles. "Good thanks. Despite being busy at work, I've managed to tackle some of the jobs in the house that I've been putting off."

I nod. "Yes, Venetia told me you were making one of the spare rooms into a cinema room."

He winks. "Yes, she says I'm having a mid-life crisis, but surely every house needs a cinema room."

Anthony heads across and laughs at the comment. "I approve of that. I mean, I make the movies and people like you keep me in business. I'd be interested to see what you've done, though. Perhaps we will copy you."

I push down the surge of anger his comment brings because I have designs on the spare bedrooms. If I get my way, they will soon be filled with children and hearing Anthony speak makes me wonder if they will ever be on the agenda.

Venetia has drifted off to talk to Miranda and I note a wistful expression in Matthew's eyes as he follows her. Not for the first time, I wonder about their relationship. They are hardly ever together and even when they are, they spend most of their time apart.

Fleur wanders over and offers us all some canapes and I smile. "These look amazing. Did you make them?"

She smiles sweetly and nods. "I did actually. I went on a day course last month at that new cookery school in town. I must say, it was such an enjoyable day. A few of the other women from the team organised it and we made canapes and drank champagne all day with a healthy lunch thrown in. We should all go; it would be such fun."

I nod and as she wanders off, Anthony raises his eyes and looks at Matthew. "If only we got to spend our days doing things that we enjoy. I think we've got this all wrong, Matt, don't you?"

Matthew shrugs. "To be honest, work keeps me sane. If I had to stay at home all day, I'd go mad."

Anthony smiles politely and heads off to talk to James and Matthew says quietly, "I hope you don't mind me asking you this, Arabella, but I don't know who else to ask."

I stare at him in surprise. "Ask me what?"

He turns so that only I can see him and says in a worried voice, "It's Venetia, perhaps it's because we hardly spend any time together, but have you noticed a change in her recently?"

I glance over at my friend and see her chatting with Anthony and James. She is laughing at something they're saying and looks happy. However, I understand what he means because happy Venetia is a rare sight these days. Nodding, I lower my voice. "Have you spoken to her and asked? To be honest, she has seemed rather preoccupied lately and quite short-tempered if I think about it."

He nods miserably. "Yes, she's the same at home. I expect I'm the one to blame. I'm always working and when I come home, she's off with me. It's no wonder she's unhappy because we just don't seem to connect as easily as we used to."

We are interrupted as Anton heads over, holding a bottle of champagne.

"Refill anyone?"

We nod and hold out our glasses and Matthew says brightly, "So, what did you buy the birthday girl?"

Anton grins. "Jewellery and a holiday to the Maldives as soon as the season finishes."

Matthew looks impressed and I think back to my conversation with Fleur, where she expressed the wish that he propose soon. Slyly, I dig a little. "So, have you any more surprises lined up for her on this holiday?"

"Not really. Why, do you think I should?"

Matthew grins as I shake my head. "No, the holiday and jewellery are more than generous. It may be because I am so happy in my marriage I'm keen to see others following in our footsteps."

Anton looks shocked. "Marriage! Oh no, nothing like that. To be honest, I couldn't fit it in between seasons. Fleur's happy about how things are and so am I. Marriage would just ruin a good thing if you ask me."

Matthew nods. "You may be right. When you're dating, it seems much more exciting, more intense and as if you can't get enough of each other. As soon as the ring slides on the finger, it becomes normal, mundane and, well, lacking actually."

They must notice my face fall because Matthew says quickly, "Although that doesn't happen to everyone. Take Arabella and Anthony here. I've never met such a devoted couple. Tell us, what's your secret?"

As I glance over at Anthony, I feel a warm feeling inside. Yes, we are the lucky ones because I am more in love with him than ever, except for one thing. Brushing that aside, I smile some-what smugly, "Well, gentlemen, what can I say? The secret is lots of laughs, lots of quality time spent together and lots of sex."

The guys laugh and Anthony looks over and I grin. Yes, Anthony and I have a lot of that particular pastime planned because I've made up my mind. I am having a child and if he won't agree, then I'll take matters in my own hands and have one without his consent. An accident waiting to happen. Isn't that what they say? Well, that's about to come true because he doesn't know it yet, but Anthony's about to become a father and then everything will fall into place.

CHAPTER 5

ARABELLA

I plan my campaign carefully. Our sex life has always been good, but it's about to become amazing. I spend the next few days searching for intimate lingerie and toys to titillate the interest in the bedroom, and I'm pretty sure Anthony won't know what's hit him when I unleash my baby campaign on him.

I've decided that tonight's the night because why wait for something I've been desperate to do for some time? I don't even worry that what I'm doing is morally wrong. Anthony will soon see that this is the best for us and in the long run, will thank me for being proactive.

The only worry I have is that the pill is still in my system. It's been four days since I stopped taking it, so it may be preventing Nature from taking its course.

As I put the finishing touches to the intimate supper I've prepared, I am quite pleased with how it all looks. All around are lit candles, adding to the seductive atmosphere. I've prepared Anthony's favourite meal of steak with Parisienne potatoes and all the trimmings and as the soft, sexy music plays through the speakers set around the house, I am excited for the evening ahead.

Underneath my black silk dress is a matching set of lingerie any prostitute would be proud of. My long, dark hair has been styled much like Fleurs was on her birthday and my lips are painted as scarlet as the woman I am. A splash of my favourite designer scent in all the right places was the final touch, as I slip on my Louboutin heels and wait for the man himself to come home.

Seven o'clock comes and goes and I adjust the setting on the oven. Typical, Anthony is never normally late and usually calls if he's going to be.

I flick through some magazines while I wait and try to think about the positives that will come from this seduction scenario.

By the time 8 o'clock passes, I'm starting to get a little worried and reach for my phone. However, as I find his number, I hear the car pulling into the driveway and my heart lifts. He's here.

As I position myself in the doorway, I try to appear poised and elegant as I hold two glasses of champagne to present him with.

As the key turns in the lock, my heart races as I imagine the shock on his face when he sees what's in store.

However, the reaction that greets me isn't the one I expected because immediately I sense something bad has happened.

Anthony heads inside the house looking tired, weary, concerned, and totally devastated.

He raises his pain-filled eyes to mine and I note the surprise in his as he registers the unusual greeting.

My smile falters as I place the glasses carefully on the hall table and say with concern, "What's happened?"

He shakes his head slowly and moves toward the kitchen

without even the usual kiss and says in a grim voice, "We need to talk."

My heart bangs frantically inside me as I follow him into the kitchen and watch him dive straight for the gin bottle and pour himself almost half a glass, before looking at me through tortured eyes. "It's bad news, I'm afraid."

"Why, what's happened?"

He sighs heavily and looks at me almost apologetically. "I'm sorry, darling."

"For what?"

"For letting you down."

The alarm bells start ringing as I picture the worst and say with a tremor in my voice, "How?"

Beckoning me over to the couch, he sits down heavily and says roughly, "I've been fired."

"What!?"

He takes a large mouthful of his drink and says in a broken voice. "I no longer have a job."

I sit beside him and take his hand in my trembling one and say as gently as I can, "Tell me what happened."

He runs his fingers through his hair and puts his face in his hands. "The last couple of films I produced lost shed loads of money. I overspent and didn't follow the guidelines. I was so sure they would be successes and they flopped - big time. The studio bosses are now out for my blood because guess what… they need a fall guy which, as it happens, is me? As of now, I am no longer employed or employable because, once this gets out, no other studio will touch me with a barge pole."

The shock hits me hard and I say fearfully, "What are we going to do? We'll be alright though, won't we? I mean, you'll sort it. We could move to America. They've been headhunting you for years now."

His silence worries me more than the words he just spoke

and then he raises his eyes to mine and what I see in them strikes fear in my heart. "No, it's over. I'm done, broken, finished. I will never work in the film industry again because they made that fact crystal clear."

I stare at him in total disbelief because I can't believe what he's saying. He's mistaken, surely. I mean, this is just a bump in the road, a setback that will make us grow as individuals. A test of the hardest kind that we will pass with flying colours—won't we?

For a while, neither of us speaks and then Anthony stands and says roughly, "I'm off to bed."

I stare at him in confusion. "What, we should talk about this. You can't just go to bed and shut me out?"

He shrugs. "I can't deal with you right now, Arabella. You need to give me some space and let me work this out. Just remember, things will be very different when you wake up in the morning because this life we lead stops now. First thing tomorrow, we need to study our options and I'm sorry, but that starts with making cutbacks and realising our assets."

Before I can speak, he is out of the room and heading for the stairs, leaving me in a total state of shock.

The sweet music continues to play and the flames from the candles dance in time with it. The smell of the feast I prepared taunts me from the kitchen and as the tears slowly trickle down my face, the only emotion I have now is one of fear. Tomorrow, our lives will change and I don't like the sound of that one bit.

CHAPTER 6

ARABELLA

I don't sleep a wink all night. Anthony took himself off to the spare room, leaving me alone and afraid in our giant bed. All night long, the worry played around in my mind as I pictured our future. It hits me around one am that the house we live in may have to go. I grow cold all over as I consider moving out and into a small house in the suburbs somewhere, away from all my friends and to a life I never wanted to lead. I may have to get a job and I worry about what that would mean. I haven't worked for years ever since I married Anthony and even then, it was only as a runner for the production company he worked for, courtesy of an introduction from my mother.

As I picture my mother's disapproving face, I want to cry all over again. She will blame me for this somehow. Everything always becomes my fault and my heart starts hammering as I picture the conversation we'll have. My father will be angry and blame me for choosing to marry a failure because they only approve of success. If they see one shred of weakness, they remove themselves from it as quickly as possible.

Then there are the neighbours. What will they say when they discover I am no longer 'one of them'?

I'm not a fool and know they will cut me off. Friendships like ours don't stand tests such as these. If we lose the house, I will lose everything that goes with it and that includes my friends.

My pillow is soaked with my tears by the time the sun rises.

I hear Anthony moving around and quickly head off in search of him, hoping a miracle has occurred in the night and this was only a bad dream.

I find him in the kitchen making his usual coffee, and he nods as I join him. "You ok?"

I fold my arms around me and say in a small voice, "No, I don't think I am."

I look to him for support and crave those strong arms to wrap around me and tell me that everything will be ok. I want him to whisper his eternal love for me and tell me that nothing will change between us. I want him to tell me he has a plan to restore our fortune and that everything will be fine and more than anything, I want him to tell me he loves me because I'm not so sure about that anymore.

Instead, he shakes his head and says somewhat angrily, "I need you to draw up a list of your expenditure and we'll go through it. That country club membership must go, and I'll need your credit cards."

I stare at him in disbelief. He's being so cold, so pragmatic, and so unlike the man I married. It's as if he's lost the ability to feel and hasn't stopped for a moment to consider how this is affecting me.

He looks at me sharply, "What?"

I say nothing and he rolls his eyes. "Go on, say it. I can tell you want to."

"Say what?"

"That you're disappointed in me, hate me, anything but the vacant expression you've been wearing ever since I told you. Shout and scream, show me some emotion for god's sake because anything would be better than this."

His words wound me deeply and I stare at him with all the frustration that built up overnight. "You want me to shout and scream at you? For what? I can't see what that will achieve. We need to talk this through and search for solutions to the problem, not hold our hands up and accept what others say. For goodness' sake, Anthony, where's all the fight gone in you? You were always so full of ideas and suggestions; are you really telling me that you are just going to curl up in a ball somewhere and admit defeat? If so, you're not the man I married."

He looks at me angrily and I hold my breath as he snarls, "Shut the fuck up. Don't you speak to me like that - ever. Don't you think I've already considered everything? This didn't only happen yesterday, it happened weeks ago and I've been trying to work out the solution, so you never even needed to know. I've shouldered this burden for a while now because I saw it hurtling towards us like a nuclear missile. Things like this don't just happen overnight, you dumb bitch. They happen over time and you've been so wrapped up in your privileged life you haven't even noticed anything's wrong. Well, things are wrong and this is the end of the line, so, do what any good wife would do and don't question my judgement and do what I tell you."

He turns away and heads towards his study without a backward glance, leaving me speechless in his wake.

Did he really say those words? That man wasn't my husband. I don't recognise him at all because the way he just spoke to me made me believe he had given up on me, too. The hate that flashed in his eyes wasn't there by chance.

Anthony Adams may have lost everything, and it appears that he doesn't want what's left either.

* * *

The rest of the day is spent working out where we go from here. Anthony retreats into his study and I start cleaning as if on autopilot. As I work, I worry and nothing that comes to mind brings me comfort.

It must be close to tea time that Anthony ventures out of his study and does what I've been aching for him to do since he told me. He wraps his arms around me and pulls me close, saying gently, "I'm sorry, darling."

I say nothing and he strokes my hair, whispering, "I took my frustrations out on you and that wasn't fair. Can you forgive me?"

I nod, although I'm not sure if I do or not. His behaviour has hurt me deeply and made me see a side to him I didn't like. However, I need him more than ever now, so I cling to him and say softly, "We'll be fine, darling. We'll sort it out; we'll work a way out of this."

I'm surprised to see a gentle smile on his face as he says, "I already have."

He laughs at the surprise on my face and says happily, "I've been in talks all morning with a few of my contacts. It's early days but I'm going to report to Castletown studios tomorrow morning. They may have something for me."

The relief hits me like a tsunami and I collapse against him as the tears fall heavily. He strokes my back and murmurs, "There, there, it will be fine. Leave it with me and I'll work it out. I shouldn't have reacted like I did yesterday, but it all got on top of me. We'll be fine, trust me."

Leaning down, he kisses my tears away and I forget everything except the fact that I love him so much. Last night was hard because I felt a distance from him that shocked me and wounded my soul. Now, as we kiss, I crave his touch to remind me I'm still loved.

As he removes my clothes, I am stripped bare inside and out and as he pushes me to the ground and enters me roughly, it's what I deserve. Anthony owns me one hundred per cent and our lovemaking reinforces that. He has always been in charge because I let him. However, he can take me however he wants because only I know the secret I'm keeping. He may call the shots, but I'm calling his future.

As he explodes inside me, I grip him tighter. Yes, Anthony may believe he's the one in charge, but I'm the one who always gets what she wants. As he collapses on top of me, I experience a flutter of excitement. This is it. Anthony has just unknowingly given me what I want the most, and if we lose everything, I hope to gain something much more valuable. A child.

CHAPTER 7

ARABELLA

*T*rust soon becomes the most important word in our marriage. I have to trust that Anthony knows what he's doing, and he has to trust me to let him. The trouble is, if he knew just how little he could trust me, it would tear down the foundations of our marriage and it's doubtful they would ever be rebuilt.

I'm not sure why, but all my reasoning and common sense have gone out of the window. Every time we have sex, I am left feeling guilty that I am firmly going against his wishes and at possibly the worst time in our life. If everything comes tumbling down and I am pregnant, I may be bringing a child into an uncertain future.

We tell nobody about our predicament and it's business as usual. Today, I'm on a shopping trip with Fleur and as we browse the rails of our favourite boutique, I wonder if I should select a different size. I mean, surely, I'm pregnant by now because I've been trying to have sex as much as possible without arousing Anthony's suspicions.

Fleur holds up a revealing gold dress and says with

excitement, "What do you think? I'm guessing Anton would love this."

Nodding, I smile my encouragement. "Try it on. You'll look fabulous."

She nods. "Yes, I expect I will."

Giggling, she heads towards the changing rooms and I grab the dresses I've been considering and join her.

We take adjoining changing rooms and she says loudly, "You know, babe, I'm so excited about my holiday to the Maldives. Do you think Anton will propose?"

Thinking back to my conversation with him on her birthday, I doubt it but just say with excitement, "I hope so. It would be good to go to a wedding. I can't remember the last one I did."

She giggles and says quickly, "Maybe I should throw in something suitable for a beach wedding, just in case. You know, Anton's such a typical man, he wouldn't give a thought to the fact I need to prepare for something as big as this. Yes, perhaps we should check out that bridal shop a few doors down and see if they have anything suitable."

"Great, I love a good bridal shop."

I turn my attention to the dresses I chose and stare at my stomach critically in the mirror. It doesn't look any different. In fact, I don't feel any different and wonder if my campaign is working yet. Perhaps the pill is still in my system and will take a while to leave. That depresses me and I gaze longingly in the mirror, imagining a baby bump proudly displayed for all to see.

Sighing, I choose what I want and head out, meeting Fleur outside the curtains and she holds up the gold dress and says happily, "I'm taking this. We're due to attend an awards ceremony soon. This will be perfect on the red carpet."

As she heads off to pay, I envy her. She has no worries at

all other than Anton popping the question. Money is an endless pit for her and I must now watch every penny.

I know I shouldn't, but I suddenly feel angry. It's all Anthony's fault. How could he be so careless to gamble with our future like this? He should have done things the right way and then we wouldn't be in this mess.

Fleur calls out, "Hurry up, Arabella. I want to catch the bridal shop before Anton's back from training."

Rushing out, I make to put the dresses back and as I do, my hand curls tightly around the beautiful white dress that I imagine myself wearing in full bloom. I'm so annoyed at Anthony, I take the dress to the counter, anyway. He owes me this at least, so I smile at the cashier and take out my credit card. One dress won't break us and I'm pretty sure he's already sorted our little problem, anyway.

I watch as the cashier gently wraps the dress in tissue paper and places it carefully in the designer bag before swiping my card.

Fleur has wandered off to look at a rail of jumpers and my heart beats as I wait for the transaction to go through. I somehow already know when cashier looks up in surprise and says, "I'm sorry Madam, have you got another form of payment? There appears to be a problem with your card?"

I watch Fleur turn around with interest and blush as I produce another. "Try this one. I think the other may be an old one."

The cashier looks at me sympathetically and swipes the new card and we wait in silence. Once again, she shakes her head and says in a whisper, "I'm sorry, this one has been declined."

Fleur wanders over and says loudly, "Bloody banks. This happened to me the other week. There was some problem nationally with the software, most inconvenient if you ask me."

She looks at the cashier. "That must be what's happening here."

The cashier says nothing because she knows as well as I do that it's no bug in the system. Quickly, I say, "It's fine, can you just put it aside and I'll be back tomorrow when the problem's sorted?"

The cashier nods, but Fleur waves her hand and produces her own card. "Here, use mine. You can pay me back when you get the problem sorted."

I watch in horror as the cashier uses Fleur's card and wonder what I should do. The trouble is, I can't form any excuse, so just smile gratefully. "Thanks. I'll pay you back when we get home."

Fleur nods, "Whenever. We won't have to pay for a month anyway, not that it would matter either way."

As the cashier hands me the dress, I feel like a total fraud. Anthony warned me about this and, like a selfish idiot, I ignored him. Now I'm in a situation I can't control, and it's all because of my own stupidity.

We head outside and Fleur looks at me with excitement. "Come on, let's go and try on wedding dresses. It will be such fun."

We head to the bridal shop and once again, I envy her. Why did I take our life for granted and not prepare for something like this? If we do lose everything, I'm not sure I could cope. When you've had everything, it's a long way down to rock bottom and there's something inside my head telling me that's exactly where I'm heading.

* * *

After a fun-filled afternoon, we head home and I quickly stash the dress in my wardrobe and hope the problem goes away. Then I race around the house, looking everywhere for any money lying around that I can use to pay Fleur back. I rustle up most of it before turning to Anthony's wardrobe in desperation. He must have some notes stashed in one of his pockets, so I rummage through them all. I manage to find a few crumpled notes and congratulate myself on a well-executed plan because I now have enough to pay Fleur back without Anthony being any the wiser. As I check the last pocket, I pull out a piece of paper that I almost disregard until I see the heading. 'The Royal Hotel.'

I'm not sure why, but it makes me stop and unfold the paper and read what's written and at first I don't understand what I'm looking at.

It appears to be a receipt for an overnight stay about a month ago. It costs a huge sum of money and I can see why. The best suite of rooms, champagne, caviar and room service —for two.

As I sit on the bench in the dressing room, my heart starts pounding. I look again and the words blur before my eyes. As I cast my mind back to the date on the receipt, I remember vaguely that Anthony was away on business. He was gone overnight, but he told me it was in Manchester. This room is one of the best in London and I feel sick as I stare at it. This is no business night away judging by the itemised entries. What the hell is he playing at and who with?

CHAPTER 8

ARABELLA

*T*he next few days pass in a blur. I want to confront Anthony but am fearful of what he might say. Instead, I become the sort of person I never wanted to be, mistrustful and anxious and I can tell he notices because he withdraws from me even more. He starts coming home late and when I question him, he says it's the long hours he has to put in to prove himself with the new company.

Money is still tight and I have to ask him every time I want something. When I told him about the credit cards, he merely fixed me with a disapproving glare and told me angrily that I wasn't supposed to be spending. Instead, I have a weekly allowance that he gives me for groceries and that's it.

I've had to turn down invitations to dinner and lunches out because I have no way of affording it. I can't even go to the country club because he cancelled our membership and I am dreading telling my friends why.

The dreaded knock on the door comes early one morning as I clean the kitchen for the umpteenth time and I'm surprised to see Fleur, Miranda and Venetia standing there looking worried.

Flour says quickly, "Okay, tell us to mind our own business, but is something the matter?"

I sense the heat flooding through me as I try to control the panic her words bring. Instead, I shake my head and fling the door open a little wider. "No, whatever makes you say that? Come in and I'll make you a coffee."

They follow me inside and my heart starts thumping as I sense the inevitable questions heading my way.

As they sit around the breakfast bar and watch me prepare the coffee, Miranda says gently, "You know, if there's a problem, we're your friends and may be able to help."

The others nod and I try to brazen it out. "No, there's no problem. Why do you ask?"

Venetia says shortly, "Because you never come out anymore and there's a rumour around the country club that you had to get a refund on your membership because you were struggling financially."

I daren't look at them and merely laugh, which sounds false even to my ears. "Nonsense, we just fancied a change, that's all."

The silence speaks volumes as I sense the disbelief in the air. Luckily, the doorbell rings, distracting me from any more awkward questions, and I smile apologetically. "I'm sorry, I won't be a minute."

Closing the door carefully behind me, I head to open the front door, sure it's the package I've been expecting from Harrods. Once again, I guiltily remember the gift voucher I used to buy myself the fabulous new pair of Jimmy Choo shoes that I needed to cheer me up.

When I open the door, I'm surprised to see two men standing there who glare at me with hard expressions.

"I'm sorry. May I help you?"

One of them holds a clipboard and says loudly, "Arabella Adams?"

I nod and step outside, pulling the front door closed behind me and say in a whisper, "Yes."

He consults his clipboard and says, "We've come to repossess your car. Can you grab us the keys and sign this form and we'll be on our way?"

I stare at him in shock before grabbing the clipboard and frantically reading the words before my eyes. "This can't be right. You've made some sort of mistake; you can't repossess something that's been paid for."

The men share a look and the other one says kindly. "I'm sorry madam, but we can. You see, this is on a list of items that are to be returned to the creditors. Your husband agreed that this will be taken as part payment against his own vehicle. We have already secured the Bentley, but now we need the Porsche. Perhaps you should call your husband and he will confirm what we say."

Nodding, I step back inside and meet Fleur heading towards me. One look at my face and she grabs my arm and pulls me into the living room, closing the door behind her. She says in a whisper, "Tell me, Arabella. I won't tell anyone else. Let me help you. I can tell something's up and no amount of denying it will change my mind."

Perhaps it's because she's being so kind and I really need a friend right now. I burst out crying and sob, "They want to repossess my car."

Shaking her head, she holds out her phone and says calmly, "Phone Anthony. He'll know what to do."

I nod gratefully and dial his number with shaking fingers. He sounds surprised when he answers because, to my knowledge, Fleur has never called him.

"Hi, Fleur, how can I help?"

"It's me, Anthony, we've got a problem."

There's a short silence before he says urgently, "What's happened?"

"Some men are here to take my car. They told me you already know about it."

Once again, the silence emphasises the distance between us and then he says in a broken voice. "Give them the keys. I'll explain when I get home."

I cut the call and turn to face Fleur with frightened eyes. "It's true."

The look she gives me couldn't make me feel any worse as I see the sympathy in her eyes. Gently, she takes my arm and whispers, "Ok, do what you have to and I'll distract the others. I'm sure it's just a blip and we can sort it; don't worry, you're not on your own."

Nodding sadly, I head off to get the keys as my heart breaks. This is so real. It's happening and soon I won't be able to disguise it anymore. The trouble is, I'm in unfamiliar territory and don't know what to do about it.

Fleur heads back to the kitchen and I hand over the keys to my precious car. Once I've signed the papers, I take a copy and the men throw me a sympathetic look before walking away. As I close the door, the walls close in on me. This is only the beginning; I know it is, and yet nothing prepares me for what's heading my way on the horizon.

The faces of the other women tell me I need to confess. It's obvious they realise something is up and to be honest, I'm too tired to try to cover it up anymore.

Fleur looks worried as I say with a sigh. "I've got something to tell you."

They stare at me expectantly as I say sadly, "Anthony lost his job along with our savings. He's got another job, but I think we owe so much it will take a while to sort the mess out."

Miranda looks shocked and says sweetly, "You poor thing, that's terrible. Is there anything we can do? Possibly James can help?"

Fleur rolls her eyes. "Only if it involves the court. I hardly think they need a Barrister, Miranda. No, they need money, and fast by the sounds of it."

Miranda looks cross. "Don't be so quick to dismiss his services. Perhaps Anthony can sue for wrongful dismissal. I'll ask James later on tonight."

Venetia looks shocked. "That's terrible."

I nod. "It is. The trouble is, that's not everything."

They gaze at me expectantly and I wonder whether to say anything at all, but now I've started with the confessions, I can't stop. "I think I may be pregnant and am worried that Anthony's having an affair."

You could hear a pin drop in the room as the horrified faces stare at me with total disbelief.

Fleur stares around her, shaking her head and Miranda reaches over and takes my hand. Venetia, however, looks angry and hisses, "Disgusting. I can't believe it. What makes you say that—the affair, I mean."

"I found a hotel receipt for a fancy London hotel when he told me he was on business in Manchester. From the details, it appears he had room service for two, including champagne and caviar. That doesn't sound like a business meeting to me, does it you?"

They all shake their heads and Miranda says gently, "Are you going to confront him?"

I stare at my friends and see the pity mixed with excitement in their eyes. This gossip is like gold dust to them and I'm under no illusions that they are revelling in it.

I shrug. "I haven't decided yet. Anyway, I can't tell him I'm pregnant because it would destroy whatever relationship we are clinging to."

Fleur says sharply, "Why?"

Sighing, I run my fingers through my hair with distraction. "Because he told me no children. He doesn't want them yet, and he could be right. Anyway, I may not be pregnant and have probably just been incredibly stupid and should come clean and confess. The secrets that are destroying my marriage tell me they're not worth hanging onto. Perhaps I should deal with all the bad news once and for all."

The others nod in agreement and Miranda says softly, "Whatever happens, you have us. If you need somewhere to escape to, we have a spare room with your name on it."

Fleur reaches out and takes my hand. "Same. You're not on your own, babe."

Venetia nods. "Yes, I expect you should talk it through. It may be the best time to get it all out in the open."

She looks at her watch and pulls a face. "Sorry, ladies, I must dash. I have a flight at ten and need to change. I'll be away for a few days, but text me if you need to, Arabella. Don't worry, we're all here for you night or day."

I smile gratefully and the others jump up to follow her. Fleur hugs me warmly and whispers, "Tell him. It's for the best, and I'm sure it will make you stronger."

Miranda nods. "Secrets are like a cancer. Leave them and they destroy. Cut the cancer out and move on with your life."

As she says the words, I notice a sadness in her eyes that isn't there for me. There's something troubling my friend and even in my darkest hour, I can see she has demons of her own.

However, I have no time to dwell on Miranda's problems because I've made up my mind. Tonight, I'm going to confront Anthony about the hotel and to hell with the consequences.

CHAPTER 9

ARABELLA

I am so nervous as I wait and practice what I'm going to say a million times over and when the key enters the lock and I hear it turn, my stomach turns with it. This is it, confession time and I'm not sure what the outcome will be.

I notice Anthony looking tired and worried as he heads inside and immediately, I can tell something has happened. He looks at me with such a worried look; I swear my heart stops beating for a fraction of a second.

There are no pleasant greetings as he says roughly, "Come and sit down, Arabella."

My legs shake as I move to sit with him on the couch, noting that he doesn't even ask for his usual gin and tonic.

He kicks off his shoes and loosens his tie and puts his head in his hands and my heart thumps as he says in a dull voice, "I haven't been feeling well lately and thought it was due to the stress I'm under, so I went to see Doctor Edmonds."

His words shock me because they weren't what I

expected. With fear, I say with a tremor to my voice, "What did he say?"

He sighs. "They've found something in my bowel. They think it may be cancer."

The screams start in my mind as I struggle to comprehend what he's saying. "Cancer?" I whisper, barely able to say the word we all dread.

He nods. "Yes, I must go in for an operation in two weeks' time. At least they're acting quickly, which is a good thing, I suppose, but it's still a shock."

As I take his hand, I squeeze it gently as the tears fall. "I'm so sorry, darling."

He nods. "Listen, don't worry about me. I'll be fine. It's just another challenge to face and another obstacle to overcome. Work has been good about it and given me time off for the operation. Until then, I'll be working longer hours to make sure everything's set for my absence."

I say angrily, "Couldn't they give you a break? You shouldn't be working at a time like this. It's not right."

Anthony yells angrily, "For goodness' sake, Arabella, don't you realise how far up shit creek we are? Of course, I must work long hours because this job is the key to our future and the last thing I need is you whining on when I need your support right now. Just put up and shut up because I am going through some serious shit at the moment and don't need a nagging wife to come home to."

He storms out of the room, leaving me gasping in disbelief. Did he really just speak to me like that? He tells me he has a life-threatening illness and when I offer him emotional support, he calls it nagging.

I can't get my head around what is happening and remember I was going to confront him about the hotel room. I realise now I can't broach the subject, because more stress is the last thing Anthony needs right now. I put my hands on my stomach and wonder if a little life is forming inside it. Have I been foolish and gone full steam ahead with something that will ultimately end badly? The walls are closing in on me, and I don't know where to turn. How has this all happened so quickly?

Suddenly, Desdemona Fortune's words come back to haunt me. Beware the Ten Commandments. Has Anthony committed adultery? Is that what she was trying to warn me about? Maybe she was right to warn me because my life has fallen into a big black hole that appears to have no way out. Perhaps this is rock bottom and we can find a solution to all our problems because the only thing I have left right now is hope and faith in God.

CHAPTER 10

ARABELLA

*A*nthony has already left when I wake the next morning. With a heavy heart, I head downstairs to make some breakfast and stare gloomily into space as the silence suffocates me. This house seems even larger than normal, if that's possible, and I've never felt so lonely. There is plenty of time to dwell on what may happen because I have nothing to do all day and no money to go out. I don't even want to speak with my friends because I can't bear their pitying looks. Then it hits me… I should get a job.

Why didn't I think about it in the first place? Of course, I need to earn some money to help out and sitting around on my backside all day helps nobody.

I'm scared, yet excited and think about what I could do. I never had to work because I met Anthony on my first job out of university. We fell madly in love and were married within months. I gave up my job to care for him and never looked back.

The doorbell rings, interrupting my thoughts, and I head towards it with a new spring in my step. As I open it, I see Fleur looking worried. "I'm sorry to stop by, Arabella. I was wondering if you managed to speak to Anthony about the hotel."

I actually forgot I told them, and it takes me back for a moment before I shake my head and pull her inside. Quickly, I fill her in on what happened last night, and she stares at me in total shock. "Oh my god, that's terrible, poor Anthony."

I nod miserably. "I know. It couldn't have come at a worse time."

Fleur looks near to tears as she says softly, "Please tell me what I can do to help."

I smile and then something occurs to me and I say with excitement, "Listen, Fleur, I've decided I need to get a job to help out. Do you happen to know of any going?"

Fleur looks a little shocked and shakes her head sympathetically. "Wow, that's bad news, babe. I can see why you need one though. Let me think for a minute."

I make her a coffee while she consults her phone, which apparently holds the answers to every question life throws at her. After a while, she looks up triumphantly. "Got it. Do you remember Darren, the super-fit hunk of a trainer we know and lust after?"

I nod and she grins. "Well, he was telling me that Rachel from the reception at the country club is leaving next week and they haven't even bothered to start advertising. If you like, I'll ask him to put in a good word for you, but it would mean working in a place you were previously a member of."

I shrug. "It wouldn't bother me. I'd be so grateful."

She grins excitedly and I watch as she dials a number and then says brightly. "Hey Darren, it's Fleur… yes, fine, thank you… um…yes…" She giggles and I note a little flush creep across her cheeks and stare at her pointedly. She grins and says softly, "Anyway, I don't suppose you'd do me a favour, babe?"

She giggles again. "No… nothing like that. Do you

remember when you told me about Rachel leaving? Yes… um, why don't you put in a good word for Arabella? Um… I know… um… yes… great, would you? I'd be so grateful."

She giggles again and I roll my eyes, honestly.

She hangs up and looks at me with a telltale brightness to her eyes. "It's sorted. He's there today and has promised to put a good word in for you."

I stare at her with amusement and her face flushes prettily. "What?"

I smirk and mimic her. "Oh, Darren giggle, giggle, giggle…"

She grins and shrugs. "So what? He's a friend with possible benefits. Not that I would ever act on them, of course. I mean, have you seen Anton lately?"

She starts fanning herself with her hand and we giggle like school girls. Yes, Fleur has it all it seems and not for the first time I'm jealous of my friend. However, she has proven to be a good one and of all of them, she is the one who appears to care the most. I hope it all works out for her because Anton would be a fool not to snap a ring on that perfect finger – sharpish.

As soon as she leaves, I busy myself with cleaning the house for the umpteenth time since this drama unfolded. I sing along to my favourite songs as I work, feeling quite upbeat for once. A job - why didn't I think of it before? This could be the making of me and it's taken something so catastrophic to happen to bring me to my senses.

When the doorbell rings, I don't give it a second thought as I head to answer it. However, I wish I hadn't because as soon as I do, I wish I could slam it shut because darkening my doorstep is the unwelcome sight of my parents.

Patricia and Hugo Armstrong are two of the most self-centred, egotistical, supercilious people I have ever met, that unfortunately also happen to be my parents. My heart sinks as I register the look they throw me because it takes me back to my childhood and the time I used to spend with them. Luckily, those times were rare because they did everything in their power to keep me at arm's length, which makes me wonder why they've taken it upon themselves to visit now.

My mother raises her well-plucked eyebrow and says in her clipped way, "Aren't you going to invite us in, darling? Anybody would think you were raised with no manners?"

Holding the door open, I say politely, "Of course, please come in, it's good to see you."

I wonder when lies like that began to roll so effortlessly off my tongue. We all say the things expected of us but I'm guessing they know I don't mean it, every bit as much as I realise they don't mean anything good they ever say to me.

As soon as they are inside, I notice them both gaze around and then share the look I remember from my childhood - the one where they find me severely lacking and I sigh inside. "Please come through and I'll make you a drink."

As they follow me to the kitchen, I'm unsettled. Why are they here and especially now? I'm having probably the worst time of my life and a visit from them is the last thing I need right now.

As I fill the kettle, I say with false brightness, "This is an unexpected pleasure. I never knew you were home."

This is actually true because the last I heard, they were at their villa in Florida and I'm surprised when my father says, "Anthony called us."

I turn to stare at them in shock and he says abruptly, "He told us all about the problems you're having and said you were struggling. He thought it may be a good thing if we came to stay for a while to help you through a difficult time."

My mother adds, "Yes, such a kind and considerate man. He is having to shoulder so much and one would hope he could rely on the strength of his wife at a very trying time, not having to prop her up and deal with her welfare while trying to deal with an intolerable situation himself."

She looks at me with a hard expression and says with disappointment laced in her voice, "Mind you, you were always unreliable and never dealt with the problems life threw at you, isn't that right, darling?"

My father shakes his head. "The trouble is, you have never had to. I blame us, Patricia. I mean, we wrapped her in cotton wool and never allowed her to experience the real world. Maybe we spoiled her too much."

I sense my blood boiling, as is usual, after five minutes in their company. That's not unusual, but what is, is the fact that Anthony went behind my back and invited them. How could he? He knows I hate and despise my parents with a passion. What's he playing at?

By the time I've made them their usual decaffeinated coffee and peppermint tea, I'm at the end of a very short tether. They have managed to run me down with every word spoken and remind me why I never call them, let alone invite them here. Now it seems they are here to stay and I feel the walls closing in on me. My life has changed in a matter of weeks and that damned fortune teller was right—it's a nightmare.

PART II

FLEUR

CHAPTER 1

FLEUR

"*B*abe, hurry up or you'll be late for training."

"I can't find my car keys."

"They're on the tray by the door where they usually are."

"Ok, got them."

I head out to the hallway and as I see Anton, my heart flutters as it always does when I catch sight of him. Pure perfection made up of solid muscle with dreamy good looks crafted by Angels. How did I get so lucky?

He grins as he sees me. "Thanks, babe. What are your plans today?"

I shrug and move into his arms as I always do before he leaves the house and plant a soft kiss on his lips. "Mm, you taste of me, babe."

He pulls me tighter against him and murmurs, "The best in the world. You're too tempting to ignore, and I'll get in trouble if they discovered I'd broken the no sex rule before training."

Giggling, I press my body against him and he groans, "Stop it, babe. You know I'm running late and this isn't fair."

I smile sweetly. "I'm only reminding you of what's waiting at home when you see all those girls will be waiting to take my place when you show up at the training ground."

Anton shakes his head and smiles, "No worries there, nobody can hold a candle to you. You know you're the only girl for me."

He winks and heads out of the door and as it closes behind him, I sigh inside. He always says everything I want to hear except one thing. I am so desperate to become his wife, but he doesn't appear in any hurry to make it official. Instead, I live under a cloud of uncertainty because he lives with temptation every day of the week. Anton Richardson is at the top of his game and with the weekly pay he receives, accompanied with looks that should be illegal on a man, I have my work cut out in keeping him.

Feeling a little unsettled, I head into the kitchen to fix my breakfast. As usual, it consists of a few pieces of fruit and some low-fat yoghurt. I may have an amazing figure but I have to work extremely hard at keeping it that way, which reminds me Darren's due later to put me through my paces.

As I think about Darren Hodges, my heart flutters a little and the excitement grips me. A hot load of trouble is Darren because he appears to be crafted from the same mould as Anton and just the sight of his hard, toned body doing strange things before my eyes is enough to send me delirious. I know I should be immune to other guys when I have such a fine one of my own, but I can't help it. There is something about Darren that sets my pulse racing and the woman in me panting. I try not to think about it, but as usual, it's never far from the surface. Sighing heavily, I think about the man that just left. I love him with all my heart and would do absolutely anything for him, but I must face the fact that I'm not sure Anton is as into me as much as I am him.

We may have just had morning sex, but that's getting

increasingly rare these days. We appear to have fallen into the category of twice a week and only when I instigate it. It bothers me a lot because I need sex like a drug and spend most of the time dealing with my urges myself, which is worrying when you consider the man that shares my bed. It makes me wonder if Anton really fancies me at all because thinking about the way Darren looks at me gets my pulse racing and makes all rationality leave the building. I would never act on it though. Why would I? Darren has made it crystal clear that he wants me, but I've kept him at arm's length because I love Anton. In fact, I want nothing more than to make this work and start our lives together as a married couple. I just need him to propose and everything will slot into place.

Sighing, I head upstairs to get ready. This morning I'm heading out for some retail therapy because I've decided to buy some more sexy lingerie in a bid to spice up our sex life. Perhaps when the season finishes and we head to the Maldives, Anton will relax a little and become the man I know he is under the stress of being an athlete at the top of his game. It can't be easy and the expectations are high. Yes, Anton is living under so much pressure, which reinforces that he needs a strong woman to make everything better when he returns home at night.

As I get ready, I glance out of the window and notice two people waiting at Arabella's front door. By the looks of them, they could be her parents because even from across the small cul-de-sac, I can see the resemblance. I think about Arabella and worry about my friend. What has happened to her doesn't bear thinking about. Not only are they facing financial ruin, but Anthony appears to have gone 'over the side' as they say, and I wonder who the mystery woman is. If it were me, I'd be a nervous wreck, and I have a new respect for Arabella. When she told me about Anthony's illness, my blood ran cold. They are serious problems that make my own appear shallow in comparison, but then again, perhaps this is just the calm before the storm because I can't stop thinking about what that stupid fortune teller said.

When I cast my mind back to that day, my heart starts thumping. She was so frightening and I'll never forget the gleam in her eye when she told me my world was about to end. Who says that? Who looks at another human being and tells them, slightly hysterically, that she can see devastation in their future and so much pain I may never recover? Just thinking of it now gives me a headache and as for the Ten Commandments, what on earth was she going on about? I quickly googled them as soon as I got home and the only ones that applied to me were taking God's name in vain. I really must stop that and have false gods. It's no secret I worship Justin Timberlake, but that's surely not what she meant.

I know I don't go to church and regularly go shopping on a Sunday, but quite frankly I'm at a loss to think of any others that would affect me.

Sighing, I pull on my favourite Chanel dress and spray my favourite perfume. Yes, a morning spent shopping is just what I need to distract myself from my problems.

CHAPTER 2

FLEUR

I hear the car pull up in the driveway and my heart starts beating furiously. Darren's here.

I check my appearance in the oversized mirror in the hallway and feel happy with the person looking back at me. Yes, Fleur Grady is looking good. She's at her peak and ready to be put through her paces by a man who would make the Devil sell his own soul to him.

My heart thumps as I head towards the front door and I plaster a welcome smile on my face and open it, revealing the super sexy personal trainer waiting on the other side.

"Hey, Fleur, you're looking good."

I smile. "Thanks, Darren. I hold you responsible for that."

He grins cheekily and the nervous flutter inside that merely looking at him brings. He is everything girls dream about and more. Slightly messy hair, sitting on top of a sculptured face, set with twinkling blue eyes. His body is hard and muscle-bound with sexy tattoos decorating arms that make me yearn for them to wrap around me and keep me safe. Darren has a habit of making a woman feel like a goddess because he looks at them as if they are the most desirable woman in the world. It's a heady combination that could make a woman ditch her principles in a heartbeat if that look was directed at them. The trouble is, that look is always directed at me and I know if I gave him the right amount of encouragement, he would be all over me like a dog in heat.

"Follow me, babe, where do you want me today?"

I giggle as he growls, "Don't tempt me. You know you're such a tease."

I laugh. "Takes one to know one."

He grins and I laugh softly. Yes, we're two of a kind, Darren and me. Both of us realise the effect we have on the opposite sex and put us together in a room and the sparks always fly.

We head to the gym that Anton had purpose built in the garden and I watch as Darren deposits his bag on the floor and regards me with a look that could strip paint. "Ok, babe, let's warm-up."

I swallow hard as Darren starts putting me through my paces and wonder if I will make it through this hour with my dignity intact. I'm not sure why, but it's becoming increasingly difficult to drive him from my mind because where Anton doesn't appear to want me, it's extremely obvious that Darren does and I use that fact to make myself feel better.

One hour later and I'm exhausted and not only from the extreme workout, either. Being so 'up close and personal' with Darren is seriously messing with my mind, so it's with considerable relief that I stretch out and say thankfully, "Here, let me make you a coffee or something as a thank you."

Darren grins and says suggestively, "I'll take the something."

Rolling my eyes, I head toward the house with Darren walking by my side. He looks around him and says with approval, "You have a lovely home, Fleur. I'm not surprised, though; you take care in every aspect of your life and I wouldn't expect your home to be any different."

I smile and say lightly, "Where do you live, Darren?"

"Chessington."

"What, the theme park and zoo?"

He grins. "Some may say I'm an animal but no, near to it, though. Have you ever been?"

I picture the local theme park and say with a grimace, "Not really my thing, babe."

He laughs. "What is your thing?"

I shrug. "I don't know, fancy restaurants, parties, shopping..."

Laughing, I turn to look at him. "Ok, I hold my hands up. I'm the shallow one here."

Darren nods. "You said it. Anyway, don't knock it until you've tried it. If you like, I'll take you to the theme park and show you what you've been missing."

I stare at him in surprise. For all our flirting, he's never actually extended an invitation to me and I'm a little on edge. He takes my hesitation as an opportunity and places his hand on my arm, sending sharp bolts of longing through my body as I feel his touch. He says gently, "I mean it, Fleur. I would love to spend some more time with you. You intrigue me and I like what I see."

For once I am lost for words and then, as luck would have it, Anton returns early and I peer up as he heads out of the bifold doors towards us. Darren drops his hand away and looks at him curiously as Anton nods. "Hey, I'm Anton. You must be Fleur's trainer."

My breathing intensifies as the two men in my life meeting for the first time and say quickly, "You're back early, babe. Is everything ok?"

Anton nods. "Yeah, they let us go early for once, so I came home to finish what we started earlier."

My face flushes as Anton looks at Darren pointedly and Darren coughs nervously. "I'll leave you to it. Nice to meet you, Anton. I'll see you on Monday morning, Fleur."

I catch Anton's eye and he looks kind of angry, which excites me. Anton's jealous. It's obvious. Feeling quite happy about that, I see Darren out and as soon as the door closes, Anton pulls me towards the stairs with an urgency I haven't seen for some time and growls, "You're coming with me."

Struggling to keep up, I say breathlessly, "But I must stink. I haven't showered."

Anton says darkly, "I want you just the way you are, the dirtier the better."

Wow, this is so hot. I've never seen Anton like this. It's as if he's possessed and I'm not going to lie, I love it.

Anton pounces on me like a wild animal and starts ripping my clothes off in haste as soon as we reach the bedroom. He kisses me hard and fast and, for want of a better word, devours me. He makes love to me like he never has before, rough, hot and dirty, and I absolutely love it. He has a desperation to him that makes my heart sing because I know what this is – he's jealous. He saw me with another man who obviously wants me and it's sent him over the edge. Who knew that was all it would take?

As Anton pounds into me, he grips my wrists hard and holds me down. He thrusts inside like a man possessed and snarls, "You're mine, all mine."

I gasp, "I'm yours, babe, only yours."

Something about him is different. Gone is the sweet caring man I love and in his place is a man intent on only one thing, proving himself. There is no care, no love, and no gentle coming together of two people in love. This is brutal, hot and sexy and to be honest, I'm not sure what I think of it.

Anton climaxes with such intensity it leaves my legs shaking and the burn ripping through my entire body and I feel sore, ravaged and strangely used. As he pants beside me, something bothers me. What was that? It was so out of character and I should have loved every minute, but I didn't. I'm not sure why but it was as if he was using my body to drive some kind of demon out and shaking. I turn my face to the wall and squeeze my eyes tightly shut. The bed dip as he leaves me without our usual cuddle and he says roughly, "I need a shower."

As I hear the water run, I stare at the ceiling and wonder what the hell just happened.

CHAPTER 3

FLEUR

*I*t's been two days and Anton has reverted back to the man I love. There's been no mention of what happened and I'm happy to just put it down to jealousy and hope it never happens again.

I peer at myself critically in the mirror and say, "Is this is too dressy for dinner with the neighbours?"

Anton looks up and my mouth waters at the sight of him. He is dressed in tight-fitting, black ripped jeans and a top that clings to his extremely athletic body. His hair is still damp from the shower and the aftershave I love wafts across the room towards me.

He smiles appreciatively, "You look beautiful, babe."

Smoothing down the white silk dress, I have to agree with him. Yes, I love to shop and when it rewards me with fantastic clothes such as this dress, I can see why I indulge my passion so much. This dress looks a million dollars and gives me a confidence I never really had growing up. I was one of three children raised by a single mother in a tower block near Croydon. We never had money for clothes and, being the youngest, all of mine were handed down by my sisters. It was only when I started modelling that I got my break and met Anton when I did some work at his club. I've never looked back since and even though I spend a lot, I haven't lost sight of that girl I was who started with nothing. I still do the odd modelling job that pays well but largely I spend Anton's money, which should bother me, but it doesn't. No, Anton couldn't care less because he earns a fortune every week and likes me to reap the benefits. He's told me often enough, so any concerns I had at the beginning are long gone.

I know what people think of me and yes, it does hurt. I suppose that's why I spend so much time trying to be a good friend and neighbour. I want them to see that I'm not just some gold digger out for what she can get. All I want is to marry Anton, have lots of babies and care for them all for eternity. It helps that we live such a charmed existence, but having come from nothing that doesn't scare me as much as it obviously does Arabella who has never had to struggle.

Once again, I worry about her. I know she's not coming tonight because her parents are here and Anthony's working. Making a note to check on her tomorrow, I turn to Anton and say, "Do you know if Venetia and Matthew are coming?"

He shrugs, "Why would I? You know more about the neighbour's movements than I do. I just turn up when told."

He grins as I roll my eyes and glimpses at his watch. "We'd better go. We're already ten minutes late and they'll have a seizure if anyone's even a minute late."

Laughing, I nod, "You're right there. I've never met such an anal couple in my life."

Taking Anton's hand, we head toward Miranda and James's house. A mirror image of ours from the outside but very different inside. Whereas ours is chic and modern, theirs is absolutely stuffed with antiques and furniture that wouldn't look out of place in the last century. It always creeps me out a bit when we go there because, like James, the whole house feels stuffy and forbidding.

Miranda is the sweetest woman I know, but James scares me. He's a very educated man and a Barrister and is probably used to dealing with a certain type of person. Both Anton and I are self-made, and I always think he looks down on us a little. James has led a privileged life, as has Miranda. They both attended private schools and then university, resulting in a high-flying career. Miranda used to be a legal secretary, which is how she met James, but gave that all up when they married, as appears the norm in The Chase, except for Venetia.

Anton is strangely silent beside me, and I know why. Like me, he is like a fish out of water around James and is probably dreading this evening, as am I.

Squeezing his hand, I whisper, "Don't worry, babe. Lots of alcohol will get us through this ordeal."

He laughs softly. "I'll hold you to that. I'll need to drink his dusty cellar dry to survive dinner with those two."

I have to agree with him. Miranda and James are hard work and it was only because I couldn't think of an excuse not to come that we're here at all.

Miranda answers the door dressed in a floor-length, pale blue dress that complements her brown bob. She's a pretty girl but wears minimal makeup and always seems to lack confidence, so I say emphatically, "You look amazing, Miranda, I'm loving that colour on you."

We kiss on the cheek and she blushes prettily as Anton repeats the compliment. "Oh, this old thing; I've had it years."

As she turns to guide us inside, I whisper to Anton, "Old dress, my arse. I've seen that same one at Stella McCartney, and it's not cheap."

Anton grins as we follow Miranda through their dark, dismal hallway, to the living room where I peer around with dismay. A fire burns in the grate, but that's the only thing this room has in common with ours. Huge leather chesterfield sofas dominate the room, surrounded by various huge wooden bookcases that hold many old leather-bound books. The threadbare rugs are expensive but could use a good clean and the oil paintings on the wall have individual lights above them, reminding me of those stately homes on the television. I shiver as I struggle to breathe in the dark, severe-looking room and then I notice James standing by the fire with a glass in his hand, watching us and smile politely.

"Hi, James, it's lovely to see you. It's good of you to invite us."

I kiss him on the cheek and watch Anton shake his hand. I can tell Anton is uncomfortable around James because he is wearing the closed expression he reserves for people he doesn't know. However, James just smiles broadly and booms, "Lovely to see you both. Now, what can we get you to drink?"

Miranda nods and I smile, "A white wine please."

He turns to Anton. "How about you? Are you allowed the hard stuff tonight?"

Anton nods and I grin to myself. Yes, Anton will need a whole bottle of the hard stuff to survive an evening in James's company.

Miranda soon hands us our drinks and I say with surprise, "Are we the only ones? I thought Matthew and Venetia may be around."

She shakes her head. "No, Venetia's away and Matthew's working. Something about a strike expected early next week, so he's in meetings to try to avoid the certain chaos it would cause."

James looks thoughtful. "I still don't understand his position in that airline."

Miranda rolls her eyes. "Oh, for goodness' sake, James, I've told you many times, Matthew is the chairman of Venus Air. He runs the whole bloody thing."

He looks suitably impressed, and Anton says, "How did he meet Venetia?"

I answer, "He was on one of her flights and they hit it off. She told me she didn't even realise he was her boss until he confessed after the third date."

James laughs. "That must have come as quite a shock."

Miranda smiles dreamily. "I think it's romantic."

James snorts. "Stupid bloody woman. You think a dog advert is romantic. Romance gets you nowhere. I should know, I've participated in enough divorce proceedings to witness first-hand what happens when the romance dies. No, companionship is the answer and staying on the same page."

He fixes Anton with a shrewd look. "What about you, Anton? Surely you agree with me?"

Anton looks uncomfortable, so I intervene. "No, Anton's all about the romance, isn't that right babe? I mean, why settle for anything less? Look at us. We're still in the first flush of love and have it all to look forward to. We're in no hurry to become that boring couple who finish each other's sentences and wear matching clothes. No, Anton and I love the romance that goes with finding your soulmate, isn't that right, babe?"

Anton nods and pulls me close to his side and smiles sexily, "Of course it is, you're spot on. Why rush something amazing?"

I catch Miranda's eye and she smirks, which annoys me. Ok, so all my friends know how desperate I am to move this on to a more stable relationship, but James has seriously pissed me off and I would rather what Anton and I have than what my friend has. To be honest, she looks totally miserable all the time, and he is hardly ever here.

As I grip Anton's hand just a little tighter, I'm glad we're as close as we are and I hope nothing ever changes that.

CHAPTER 4

FLEUR

*A*fter dinner, Miranda smiles and nods towards the door. "Fleur, I would love your opinion on something. Would you mind?"

I stare at her in surprise and don't miss the blind panic enter Anton's eyes and I know why. He and James are chalk and cheese and he will find it difficult to maintain a conversation with the stuffy barrister and I feel bad about leaving him. He notes my discomfort and smiles, "It's ok, you go, I'll be fine."

James snorts. "Of course he will. Listen, I've got some seriously good brandy in my study, Anton. How about we break it open and leave the girls to it?"

Miranda nods happily. "Yes, that would be great. I'll rustle up some coffees shortly and call you when they're ready."

As we all split up, I'm curious what she wants and follow her up the huge staircase that dominates the centre of the house.

Miranda's house is completely different from ours in its interior, but the same in its layout. She guides me towards the rear of the house, where the master bedroom overlooks the rather large garden. Although it's dark, I know that Miranda loves her garden, and it's a horticultural paradise. Every species of rose appears to grow in it and she has a vegetable garden and greenhouse where she grows her own plants. On the other hand, ours is practical and more modern, with evergreen ornamental trees and a large swimming pool taking a good part of it up. Yes, we are very different, but for one thing, we both love to shop.

I follow Miranda into her dressing room and she looks at me with excitement. "Listen, Fleur, don't tell James, but this dress was a steal at Stella McCartney."

Grinning, I roll my eyes. "You don't have to tell me, babe. I knew as soon as I saw it. You forget I'm a connoisseur of fashion."

Laughing, she proceeds to whip out three large, white boxes and we pour over the contents with excitement. I gasp at the beautiful cashmere jumper and fur-lined shawl. The beautiful grey silk dress that she holds against her makes me envious and she giggles at my expression. "They're gorgeous, aren't they? James would throw a fit if he discovered how much they cost, but I absolutely had to have them. You understand how it is."

Nodding, I hold the shawl against me and sigh. "Exquisite, you must tell me where you got them from."

She lowers her voice, "Gucci."

I shake my head and she giggles. "Don't tell anyone because if James ever found out they weren't from the charity shop like I told him, he would start divorce proceedings immediately."

I peer at her with concern. "But won't he see the credit card receipt?"

She grins and says triumphantly, "No, because I paid cash."

Laughing softly, I have to hand it to her. She's a smart

one, that's for sure. I think we've all pulled off the 'this old thing' routine and I have a newfound respect for Miranda. I never realised she could be so devious and I kind of like the fact she's got one over on James.

I'm not sure how long we stay in her dressing room for, drinking champagne and trying everything on, but I suddenly remember poor Anton downstairs and say somewhat guiltily, "We should head back, we've been gone ages."

She nods reluctantly. "You're right. Let's make the coffee and find out what those boys have been up to."

As we head downstairs, the study door opens and the men come out at the same time. I feel bad as I register the pained expression on Anton's face and he smiles wearily, "Have you had fun, babe?"

I nod. "Yes, how about you?"

He smiles but I can tell he's found the evening quite arduous, so I say quickly, "Actually, Miranda, I hope this doesn't sound rude, but would you mind if we skipped the coffee? I have a migraine coming on and recognise the signs and need to get to a darkened room as quickly as possible."

I feel bad as she looks at me with concern and James says loudly, "Poor you, I used to suffer with them too. You should make an appointment with the doctor; they can sort them, you know."

Nodding, I grab Anton's hand and smile gratefully. "I will, thank you, James. Anyway, super evening and amazing company. Thank you again and you must certainly come to us next time so we can repay the favour."

Anton says his own goodbyes and I feel a little bad for Miranda, but I'm pretty sure Anton's had as much of James as he can stomach for one night and will be grateful for the intervention.

As we head home, he sighs heavily. "What would I do without you?"

Snuggling into him, I say softly, "We're a good team."

He kisses me on the head and says lovingly, "We sure are."

As we head inside our amazing home, I sigh with relief. Home at last and with the one man I love. Life doesn't get much better than this except for one thing that's missing—a wedding ring.

* * *

When I wake the next morning, I'm surprised to find the space beside me is empty, which surprises me and glancing over at the clock, I can see it's seven so I haven't overslept.

Jumping out of bed, I go in search of Anton and after a while track him down to the gym in the garden. I hear his grunts of pain as I venture inside and note the sweat dripping down his body as he seems to be almost punishing himself on the running machine.

He sees me enter the room and nods, but doesn't let up. I say with surprise, "Are you ok, babe?"

He smiles but I notice it looks strained as he says breathlessly, "Couldn't sleep, so I thought I'd get some training in. I won't be long and could murder a coffee."

I smile and move away, but am a little worried about the expression in his eyes. I know him so well and can tell that something's bothering him. If I'm honest, he's been like this for weeks now and I just put it down to the strain of waiting to see if he gets his transfer through to Arsenal.

Thinking about the possible move, I wonder if it would be such a good thing. We're settled here and both love the club he's currently in. The trouble is, football is a business, and he has been approached by another team offering him more money and better chances of starting the games. Anton's under no illusions he has to make as much money as possible while he's at the top of his game, so is seriously happy at the thought of progressing. I'm not sure I share his excitement because it would mean moving to North London and starting all over again. However, I would move anywhere to be with him and so I'll have to suck it up if it does happen.

As I wait for the kettle to boil, a text comes through from Darren. My stomach flips as I eagerly reach for the phone and hate myself for thinking of him at all. My feelings towards him need to be dealt with because nothing must get in the way of my relationship with Anton.

However, the message actually doesn't concern me and I cry out when I see he's arranged an interview for Arabella with the manager of the country club regarding the receptionist's position.

Feeling upbeat, I decide to head over there after breakfast and tell her the good news.

It's not long before Anton heads inside and I stare at him with concern.

"Is everything ok, Anton?"

He looks surprised. "Of course. Why wouldn't it be?"

"I'm not sure, but you seem kind of pre-occupied if I'm honest."

He shakes his head and looks a little irritated. "For God's sake, babe, do I have to plaster a smile on my face every hour of the day? I am allowed to switch off from time to time without having to explain myself."

I say nothing and push the coffee towards him and he sighs. "I'm sorry for snapping, but I've got a lot on my mind. The season's about to finish and then the transfer window opens. Our lives could be very different soon, and I'm not sure I'm mentally prepared for it."

Moving across, I reach for him and pull him to me gently, murmuring, "It's ok. I'm here for you no matter what happens. If you move, I move, simple. That is, if you want me to."

He pulls back and I'm amazed at the passion in his eyes as

he says emotionally, "Fleur, you are the best thing in my life, and I really don't deserve you. I'm not sure I say it enough, but I really love you and couldn't live without you. Try not to let my moods cause you concern. It's nothing and well, I will always put you first, babe."

He pulls me close and I swear I'm in shock. Anton has never said anything like that to me before—ever and I experience a tingle of excitement as I absorb what he said. Anton loves me more than anything. My heart settles and my world rights itself because that was all I needed. To feel valued and loved and, well, secure. Maybe I don't need a ring on my finger to remind me I'm loved. That was enough for me and I snuggle into him and say softly, "I love you too, babe. I always will."

Just for a moment, we stand together, holding one another. It's a sweet moment that will stay in my heart forever and at this moment in time, I am the happiest I have ever been.

CHAPTER 5

FLEUR

*A*nton leaves for training and I leave the house and make the short walk across the cul-de-sac to Arabella's. Again, her house is identical to mine and, unlike Miranda, she loves everything designer. I swear she buys something new for her home every week because there are always delivery vans parked outside from some of the premier designer home shops. She has such amazing taste. I am always jealous of her flair with the interior of her home.

However, since Anthony's confession, there have been no more deliveries because I understand money is tight and yet that is now the least of their concerns.

As I wait for her to answer the door, I'm a little nervous. I've never been good with people's illnesses. Relationship problems—yes, I could give advice all day long but this, well —its life-changing and I am in no way trained to dish out advice.

Arabella opens the door and I can instantly register the strain in her eyes as she smiles wearily and says, "Fleur, thank goodness, someone normal to talk to. Come in and I'll make you a coffee."

I follow her inside and we make our way to the kitchen, which is thankfully empty. I know her parents are still here because their large Jaguar is parked in the driveway, but I want some alone time with Arabella to check on how she's bearing up.

She smiles as I take a seat at her breakfast bar and says in a whisper, "I'm in a living Hell, Fleur. As if it's not bad enough that Anthony's ill and facing bankruptcy, my parents descended on me with their usual amount of vitriol and aggressive behaviour."

I glance at her sympathetically, and she sighs. "I keep on thinking back to that fortune teller we all went to. Despite how annoyed I was at the time; I actually think she was spot on."

"Why do you say that?"

She laughs bitterly. "Because, quite frankly, I'm about to break several of those commandments. For one, I've never respected my father and mother and am liable to murder them both at any moment. Anthony has committed adultery, I'm absolutely sure of that, and there's not an hour of the day that I don't take the lord's name in vain. I'm such a bad person and deserve all that's happened."

I stare at her with a fierce expression. "Stop talking. There is no way on earth you're a bad person, just an extremely unlucky one. You can't choose who your parents are and there's no law that says you must like and respect them. Respect is earned and from what you've told me, yours definitely don't deserve any. As for Anthony, the adultery thing is on him, if that is what really happened. Did you ever confront him?"

She shakes her head miserably. "How can I? For one thing, he's never home and always working. If he does come home, he's tired, irritable and appears to want to spend time with my parents over me. I'm not sure what I've done wrong, but whatever it is, Karma is throwing payback at me with a water cannon."

Despite the serious situation, we both laugh and then I hear, "I'm not sure what you've got to laugh about, young lady. I'd have thought you would be trying to work out a solution to your problems rather than gossiping with friends."

Startled, I glance up and see an extremely smart woman heading into the room. She is poised and immaculately dressed, with her almost white hair tied up in a chignon and her make-up apparently trowelled on. Resisting the urge to recommend she get her foundation colour tested because it appears at least three shades too dark for her skin, I say icily, "Good morning, you must be Arabella's mother. I'm Fleur, her neighbour and best friend."

I hold out my hand but she ignores it completely and looks down her nose, before saying, "Oh yes, the footballer's girlfriend. Arabella told me you were staying here for a bit."

Her eyes flash as she almost spits the words from her thin, angry lips and Arabella gasps and says in a shocked voice, "Mother, please don't be rude to my friend."

Shrugging, she moves toward the garden door and I snap, "Yes, manners cost nothing and it's evident Arabella never inherited hers from her mother. Mind you, I'm not surprised because from what I've heard, you had minimal input in her upbringing, which I can now understand was actually a blessing in disguise."

Turning to Arabella, I say sympathetically. "I see what you mean about your mother, babe. Bad luck, but at least you only have to suffer for a few more days, hopefully. Imagine living with her 24/7."

Arabella turns away and I see her shoulders shaking as her mother rounds on me angrily. "How dare you speak to me like that, you common slut? I've seen the bad press you girls get and now I know why. You may have 'made it' in your eyes, but you'll always be a common little whore from a council estate with a mouth like yours. Breeding can't be bought, my dear, and no amount of money your boyfriend may have will make up for the lack of yours. You know, I give you less than a month before he finds another plaything, and then where will you be?"

"Shut up!"

We turn in surprise to witness Arabella almost shaking with rage as she looks at her mother. "I've just about had enough of you and your superior ways. I've bitten my tongue until I think I need medical help, because these last few days have been excruciating. You have no right at all to speak to Fleur like that because she is one hundred times a better person than you will ever be. She's kind, considerate, generous and loving. All the things you sorely lack and quite frankly, I've had enough."

Her mother makes to speak and Arabella says loudly, "Just don't. I don't want to hear it. Every word out of your mouth is poisonous. All my life you've belittled me, pushed me away, looked down on me and made me feel as if I never measured up. Even when I married, you told me I'd got lucky and now, this has happened. You told me at every available opportunity that it was my fault. My fault! Was it my fault that Anthony lost all our savings and messed up his career because of his own stupidity? Was it my fault that he lied to me about spending a night in a fancy hotel with what appears to be another woman and is it my fault that he has some terrible, life-threatening illness that could end up with me as his widow? No, it bloody well isn't. In fact, none of this is my fault, so shut the fuck up and apologise to my friend for being so rude."

"Arabella!"

We all jump as the word ricochets around the room like

Indiana Jones's bullwhip. We turn towards the voice and I register a man standing there who I guess is her father, looking so angry I feel myself shaking. Her mother races across to him and cries, "Hugo, did you just hear the way she spoke to me? Deal with her at once because she has upset me greatly."

I peer at Arabella and smile when I note the defiance in her eyes as she stands her ground, and then her father says in a cold voice, "Apologise to your mother at once."

Arabella laughs bitterly, "Apologise for what exactly? You told me to always tell the truth, actually no, I don't believe it was you because you never told me anything except how disappointed you were in me. No, any lessons I've learned have been from the various nannies, school teachers and friend's mothers that I stayed with throughout my life. You know, I often wondered why you ever had me at all. What was it, a mistake? Is that what I am, a rogue sperm that dared go against the plan and ruin your lives forever?"

Her mother gasps and I watch with amusement as Hugo growls, "Enough. It's obvious you're unravelling. Are you on drugs? Is this what this is?"

Arabella looks at him incredulously and shouts, "Get out, both of you, get your things and get out. In fact, never contact me again because I have no parents. Do you hear that? No parents and sadly it appears that I never did."

The room falls silent and is thick with recriminations and years of pent up emotion. Then her mother says angrily, "I think that's a very good idea. Arabella, we've always tried to do our best for you, but you're right, we never wanted you in the first place. Yes, in answer to your question, you were a dirty little mistake that has been my cross to bear ever since it happened."

Hugo snarls, "Sophia don't."

Arabella turns white as Sophia sneers, "Don't what,

Hugo? Don't tell our loving daughter that she was a mistake. An unguarded moment with the hired help."

I stare at them in shock and Arabella turns as white as a sheet as Sylvia powers on regardless. "Yes, darling, how does it feel knowing you were the result of a dalliance with a servant? Goodness, we all make mistakes, and that was my biggest one to date. Well, obviously you take after him because the words that just spilt from your venomous lips sounded exactly like him when we sent him on his way with no reference. You should be thanking us for taking you on and giving you the best start in life. Hugo, as it turns out, couldn't have children, so we decided to keep you. It was probably a mistake because there is certainly no love there. Just a constant reminder of him. Mark Edwards, the gardener with no ambition and no pedigree. A bit of rough that scratched an itch. Well, I think you're old enough to learn the truth now, my dear, because, after that little outburst, I'm done with you. Yes, we will leave and with considerable relief at that."

She turns to her husband and says haughtily, "Come on, Hugo, our job is done here. I need to get as far away as possible from this woman who is no longer my daughter."

She turns and leaves the room and Hugo shakes his head. Turning to Arabella, I'm surprised to see what appears to be tears in his eyes, as he says softly, "I'll talk to her."

Arabella says nothing and stares at him white-faced and in total shock. Then, out of the blue, he moves across and appears to hesitate before pulling her into his arms and saying emotionally, "I'm sorry, Arabella. You should never have found out that way. It was brutal and cold."

She whispers, "It's true then?"

He nods. "Yes, my darling, I'm afraid it is. Sophia, your mother, was a little indiscreet, several times, in fact. I blamed myself because I was always working and forgave her every time."

"Every time?"

"Yes, Mark wasn't the first 'mistake'. She was wrong, though."

"About what?"

"That we never wanted you. I did. You see, I learned early on in our marriage that I could never have children. When Sophia fell pregnant, I was angry, but the selfish part of me was ecstatic. I had a child. Not of my creation, but that didn't matter to me. I loved you as soon as I saw you, but it was never going to be enough for you. Your mother is a hard woman to please and above everything and, despite what happened, I love her completely. I have spent my life trying to make her happy, so I went along with everything she said, and that will haunt me to my dying day."

I feel uncomfortable as Arabella almost collapses in his arms as she sobs uncontrollably and her father looks over at me and smiles sadly. "I'm sorry, my dear. For what Sophia said to you and for getting caught up in all of this. Look after my baby girl because I won't be allowed to."

He pulls away and lifts Arabella's face to his and smiles. "You will always be my beautiful, brave girl and I will always be your father. The dust will settle and I'll be in touch. If you need anything, call me and I'll arrange it. I love you, Arabella. I always have and nothing will ever change that. I accept we must leave; it's not doing you any favours us being here. Anthony called us to help, which surprised me because up until then, he always maintained a distance from us. Perhaps you should find out his reasons for doing so because there's something not right there."

Arabella gasps, "What do you mean?"

He shakes his head sadly and then we hear a sharp, "Hugo, I need your help packing."

Sighing, he turns away and says sadly, "Talk to him. Find out what's really going on because I've a feeling he's not being completely honest with you and as you now know, secrets can destroy everything."

He leaves the room and immediately I take his place and pull Arabella into my arms as she sobs on my shoulder. "It's ok, babe, I've got you. You're not on your own."

She says in a small voice, "What have I done?"

"The right thing. What happened here was always going to happen. You said your piece and found answers to why you've been treated the way you have. At least your father opened up to you. That was good, wasn't it?"

She smiles sadly. "Yes, despite everything, that surprised me the most. Maybe it was a good thing because at least now I know and can build on something that was always going to come toppling down."

I nod emphatically. "Today is the first day of the rest of your life. You can take charge and start building a better future for yourself away from somebody else's shadow, which reminds me why I came in the first place."

She looks at me with interest. "Why?"

"Darren texted me. You have an interview at the country club at two o'clock sharp. I'll drop you there myself so, grab a drink, shower and change into your smartest dress and take charge of your life."

I'm pleased to witness a little of the light return to Arabella's eyes as she says in surprise, "An interview, me?"

I nod and grin. "Yes, and you'll be the best god-damned receptionist that place has ever seen."

Arabella laughs. "Beware the Ten Commandments, Fleur. You just broke one of them and Desdemona will be saying, 'I told you so.'"

As the door slams, we stare at each other and Arabella laughs. "There goes another one."

I grin. "I think even the almighty himself would have broken his own rule in that case. I think you'd be forgiven for that one."

As we listen to the roar of the engine on the driveway outside, it strikes me that Arabella looks different somehow. It's as if a huge weight has fallen from her shoulders and that makes me happy. She may be at rock bottom, but she's a fighter. Perhaps she is more like her real father? I hope so because I sure as hell hope she's got none of her mother in her.

CHAPTER 6

FLEUR

I pick Arabella up at one-thirty and can tell she's nervous. She sits beside me and I say softly, "You look amazing, Arabella. They would be mad not to snap you up on the spot."

"Perhaps, but it's been so many years since I last worked, why would they employ me? I mean, I have no experience and no references and to be honest, if I were in their shoes, I wouldn't give me the time of day."

I fix her with a stern frown. "Nonsense. You are everything they're looking for. You're presentable, reliable and pleasant. You say you have no experience, but I disagree."

She looks surprised and I smile. "You've run a home for several years and kept that husband of yours organised. I've never known anyone who can arrange an event like you can and if they want experience, tell them of all the parties and days out you've organised over the years. What about your home? You keep that running like a well-oiled machine and nothing isn't recorded and filed in that state-of-the-art filing system you operate. To be honest, I've never met a person so anal about record keeping, with a weird need for meticulously filing every receipt away in its relevant section. No, you've got this, babe, and if they need a reference, throw me down as one. I'll vouch for you and it would be my pleasure."

Arabella's eyes fill with tears and I stare at her in alarm as she says softly, "Thank you."

"For what?"

"For being the best friend a girl could wish for. I realise it's not been easy for you fitting in with the rest of us and I feel bad about how we were so cold to you at first."

I fall silent because it still stings how they dismissed me at first as just another warm body to warm Anton's bed at night. I realise he had a revolving door to his bedroom when he first moved here and I suppose I've always known I didn't fit in, which is why I've made such a tremendous effort to.

Sighing, I reach over and lace my fingers with hers and say with emotion. "You're the best friend I could have wished to find. Don't feel bad about how things were at the beginning; I realise I'm a fish out of water here. Perhaps my coming here has taught all of us lessons. I like to think I've developed as a person since meeting you all. Sometimes we need to see ourselves how others see us from time to time. It makes us stronger and teaches us how to grow as an individual. Today you did just that, Arabella. I was proud of the way you stood up to your mother and you deserve only the best in life. Don't let the past drag you down. I never do and look to the future with open eyes. You're a strong woman, babe, and I will always have your back like I know you have mine."

She squeezes my hand and I have a friend for life in Arabella, which actually means the world to me. I've never fitted in because I always wanted the dream. Now I'm living it and sometimes I wonder how long it will last because now I've found it, I want to hold on to it with everything I've got because this is everything I ever wanted in life and it would be hard to see it all slip away.

As soon as we park up, Amanda disappears off for her interview and I head to the bar for a coffee. I could work out in the gym, but I'm not in the mood today because I keep on dwelling on Anton and his moods. One minute he's all over me and the next he is so cold and I wonder if he feels anything for me at all. I'm not stupid and realise he must have many temptations. Would I recognise the signs if he were being unfaithful? Probably not because I've had my fair share of temptation and now it appears to be heading my way looking hot, dangerous and like the total homewrecker he could be given a little encouragement.

"Hey, Fleur, do you mind if I join you?"

Smiling, I nod toward the seat opposite. "Hi, Darren, please do. I'd like some company."

He slides into the seat opposite and grins and I hate the way my heart starts thumping and feel the desire reaching the parts of me that should only want one man.

He leans forward and whispers, "I wish more than anything you were a single woman, Fleur."

I stare at him in shock. "Darren, stop!"

He shrugs. "I can't help it. I meet many women, all of whom make their intentions clear. Some are married, some are not. I could choose any of them, but there is something about you that sets you apart from the rest."

I grin. "Spoken like a true player."

Suddenly, he looks serious and says roughly, "I mean every word. It's tearing me up inside and I don't know why, but I can't stop thinking about you and to be honest, it's driving me insane."

I'm not sure what to say and gaze at him gently. "You do know I'm in love with Anton."

He nods miserably. "Yes. I understand nothing will come of this, but I needed to tell you at least. Maybe if things change, you will remember this conversation and come and find me. Perhaps we are meant to be together and the timing sucks. You may not even feel the same way and I'm just being a fool, but I had to put it out there. Life is short and I've always been one to seize the moment. None of us knows how long we've got and I don't want to look back and wish I'd done things differently. Call me a fool for even daring to believe a woman like you would ever be interested in a man like me, but that's what love does to you. It blinds you to fact and disguises reality. Don't think badly of me for trying, Fleur, because I just needed to say it. Now I have, I can accept that nothing changes and we are friends, trainer and client and that's fine by me."

He smiles ruefully and sighs. "Anyway, I have a class to get to and I've embarrassed you and myself for long enough. Take care and let's carry on as before with no hard feelings?"

Smiling, I shake my head. "No, no hard feelings and for the record…"

He looks worried. "For the record, Darren, if I wasn't with Anton, I'd be all over you like a rash."

I grin as he laughs. "Thanks, darling. That's good to hear."

I watch him walk away with sadness. I do love Anton, that's true. I can't help that, but I'm not so sure he loves me even half as much as I love him. Darren, on the other hand, I know he loves me. It's written all over his face. He didn't have to say what he did and, if anything, he made himself look bad by even voicing what was inside his heart. However, I have a newfound respect for the cheeky trainer because he was true to himself and who can think badly of a person about that?

It's not long before Arabella heads towards me and, by the expression on her face, she's got good news. She sits down and grins from ear to ear and says proudly, "I got the job."

I squeal with excitement and she laughs. "I can't believe it. They told me I can start next week, nine to five. Can you believe that Fleur, me a working woman earning her own money and joining the rat race?"

"I'm happy for you, babe, really I am. Maybe now your luck will change."

She shrugs. "Who knows? I suppose this is the start of a possible new life for me. If Anthony does go bankrupt, we will both need to work hard just to survive. It's a sobering thought, don't you think?"

I nod. "I know that better than most, Arabella. I may spend Anton's money as quickly as he earns it but I realise how difficult it is to earn a living. If this dream ends tomorrow, I'm under no illusions about how hard I'll fall. Sure, I could increase my modelling jobs and actively seek work. They will only be as good as long as I have my looks, so what then? No, I need to consider my future and prepare for it. If anything has reinforced that fact, it's what's happened to you."

She nods. "Yes, it shows how quickly life can change."

We stand to leave and not for the first time, I admire my friend. Despite the hard knocks thrown her way, she's still positive and looking forward. I can learn a lot from Arabella and as we head home, I'm glad I've found such a great friend in her.

CHAPTER 7

FLEUR

*A*s soon as we turn into The Chase, I see Anton's car in the driveway. I glance at the clock in surprise because I was sure he told me he would be late today, something about a medical. I drop Arabella off and then head home, feeling a little worried. What if something went wrong with the medical? His transfer hinges on his fitness and this could change everything.

As soon as I get inside, I call for him. "Anton, babe, where are you?"

The house is silent and I head into the kitchen, hoping he's there, but nothing. By the looks of things, he's been here a while because the usual mess greets me of a lunch made and then strangely abandoned. I've not known him to leave food uneaten before, so I head upstairs, calling, "Anton, are you here, babe?"

Still nothing, so I check each room looking for him because he can't be far. I notice his dressing room door open and see some of the contents spilt out over the floor but think nothing of it. He's always been messy, so it's not unusual. Perhaps he's gone for a run or is outside in the garden.

Then I look out of the window that overlooks the garden and my blood runs cold. With a sob, I turn on my heels and run as fast as I can towards the back door, my heart banging inside me with every step I take.

There's a body floating in the pool.

Wrenching open the door; I race to the pool's edge and then I start screaming and I couldn't stop if I tried. Anton is floating face down in the pool, fully clothed, and as I jump in, I cry, "Anton, oh babe, please tell me this is a joke, please."

I reach him and flip him over and the sight of the face before me will haunt me to my dying day. He's dead.

Sobbing uncontrollably, I scream for help and then try to drag his body to the side. If I can only get him to the side, I could try to revive him. I pull myself out dripping from the pool and try to haul him out, but I'm not strong enough. Nobody comes and I realise I must get help but I can't leave him but reasoning kicks in and I race inside and grab the phone and as the operator asks what my emergency is, I shout, "Ambulance, please hurry, my boyfriend's in the pool and I think he's drowned, please hurry."

The operator is calm and asks for my address, and proceeds to guide me through the next steps.

I do everything she says as if on autopilot because I can't comprehend the horror of what's happening before my eyes. Anton is dead.

Even as I battle to save him, I know he's gone. His eyes are lifeless and his body is stiff and unyielding. As I stay with him still floating in the pool, I hold on to him and sob as if my heart has broken. "Please don't leave me, I love you, please come back to me."

I don't even register the multiple bruises on his face and

body. I don't even register the dried blood on his head. I don't even register that he's fully clothed and I don't even register the help when it arrives. As the drama unfolds around me, I register nothing except the fact that Anton is dead and, as I sit shivering on the side of the pool, my world ends.

Somebody wraps a blanket around me.

Somebody thrusts a hot mug of tea in my hand.

Somebody says something, but I don't hear the words.

Somebody takes charge of the whole situation, but I don't know who because I can't see anyone other than him. The man I love who has so cruelly left me. Lying by the side of the pool covered in a sheet.

All around me they come. Police, doctors, paramedics and scenes of crime officers. The sirens fill the normally serene neighbourhood and helicopters fly overhead.

Anton is dead, which is headline news. There will be reports, television crews and managers from the club. There will be fans and family all descending on the usually serene place we call home. Life is about to change and nothing will ever be the same again because Anton Richardson is dead and as the news starts registering in my brain, I want to know why?

Hours later, I find myself sitting on the huge leather couch, wrapped in a blanket. I wouldn't go for a shower and I wouldn't speak to anyone because I don't know what to say. I just sit staring into space as, one by one, the faces change and people speak in hushed tones. Then I'm aware of a comforting hand in mine and a familiar voice says softly, "It's ok Fleur, it's Arabella and Miranda. Venetia's on her way. We've got you."

Squeezing my eyes tightly shut, a lone tear escapes. My friends. Of course, they're here. I knew they would be. It's what we do after all. We're here for each other when everything folds. Now it's my turn, and it's the cruellest one yet.

I form some shaky words. "He's gone."

Arabella squeezes my hand. "I'm so sorry, Fleur."

Miranda is crying beside me and says, "I can't believe it."

We look up as Venetia races in and crouches before me, saying roughly, "God, you poor thing. Look at you, let me help you."

Of everything that's just happened, I think her words surprise me the most. Venetia isn't one for showing her feelings. She's always been the most pragmatic of my friends and never reveals emotion. However, the catch in her voice makes me glance up and I notice the tears streaming down her face as she says angrily, "What happened? Is it really... murder?"

I stare at her in shock and tense up. Murder? It can't be.

I peer around and notice a man step forward, who says kindly, "I'm sorry, Miss Armstrong. I understand this is a difficult time, but we need some questions answered. I'm so sorry, but time is of the utmost importance and we need to discover what happened."

Nodding, I sink back and say in a small voice, "Of course, please ask me what you want to know."

He perches on the seat opposite and proceeds to ask me many questions, which I try to answer as best I can. He asks me about Anton's movements. The time he left, where he went, that sort of thing. I tell him everything and he writes it all down in his pocket notebook. Then he asks me if Anton had any enemies and I glare at him sharply. "Of course not. He's the kindest, most well-liked, funniest man I have ever met. Who would want to cause him harm? Nobody would. He's not that type of guy."

I can't bring myself to talk of him in the past tense and it doesn't go unnoticed. I see the worried looks my friends share, and it makes me angry. How can one person be here one minute and gone the next for no reason? Accidents

99

happen. I know that and say quickly, "It must have been an accident. Perhaps he slipped and hit his head on the side of the pool. That's more likely than murder. Who would murder Anton? It doesn't make sense."

The officer nods. "I'm sure you're right, Miss Armstrong. Perhaps you should get something warm on, your clothes are still wet and we don't want you catching a cold. We'll be here for a while, but I must ask if you could shower at a friend's because we need to sweep the house for evidence and nothing must be touched."

As I stare at him in disbelief, Arabella says quickly, "You can come to mine."

I allow my friends to help me up and support me on all sides as we make the short walk to Arabella's home. The usually quiet cul-de-sac is full to the brim with various vehicles and there is a huge amount of activity everywhere. I know the police have kept the film crews out, which I'm grateful for because I can't deal with anything right now. All I can think of is the sight of the man I love gazing up at me with lifeless eyes. As I walk with my friends, I feel as if I died alongside him because there is a hollow pit of emptiness where my heart used to be and it's doubtful it will ever recover.

CHAPTER 8

FLEUR

*T*hree weeks later and it still hasn't sunk in.

I stare at myself in the mirror and no longer recognise the person looking back at me. The woman I am now wears a haunted expression. She no longer laughs and she cries—a lot. Her appearance is no longer of any consequence because she doesn't care about anything anymore. But today is different. Today she has pulled out all the stops for him—Anton. Today is his day. I will walk behind him proudly and with love. I need to be strong and be the woman he would be proud of because today is Anton's funeral.

The body has finally been released and we can now bury him with as much finesse as possible because he deserves it.

I will walk behind his coffin through the many mourners who are sure to fill the church and surrounding area. I will put on a brave face because I know they will all be looking for the cracks, of which there are many.

The last three weeks have been the worst of my life and I've been lucky to have my friends and family by my side through it all. Anton's family also stayed with me and proved to be amazing throughout. His parents treated me like the daughter-in-law I aspired to be, and his sister has proved an easy listener. We have spoken long into the night about a man we all loved, and I couldn't have made it through the last three weeks without them.

Anton's club and agent stepped up and organised everything. They liaised with the police and the press and allowed me to grieve for the man I love. Nobody has said one bad word to me or insinuated that my time here is done because I know it probably is. Anton and I weren't married and so his estate will fall to his next of kin, his parents. I'm prepared for that and it's how it should be. No, I wasn't here for the money; I was here for love and now that love has gone, I must go too.

I make my way to the waiting black car and swallow hard as I see the flower-strewn hearse waiting patiently outside. It's hard to see the coffin, picturing the lifeless body of the man I love inside when he should be next to me. Fate is a cruel bitch because she has hit hard. Anton didn't deserve to die and despite the murmurs of murder, there was no evidence of that effect. There has been no resolution to something that should never have happened in the first place. The investigation is ongoing, but that can wait because today is Anton's day and I will not let him down.

It's hard facing the hundreds of people waiting and watching.

It's hard walking behind the body of the man you love who you will no longer touch, smell, and hear his voice.

It's so hard listening to that man being spoken about with many kind, emotional words and it's hard watching his body lowered into the cold ground because we were not allowed to cremate him.

However, the hardest thing of all is leaving him there as we walk away. Ashes to ashes, dust to dust are what face us all. Anton will become a valuable memory because there will be no future to speak of. As I move on with my life, he cannot. I've no doubt I will recover. I'm a survivor and will start again somewhere else, but there's an important part of me that lies with Anton in that grave—my heart.

By the time the last person leaves, I am exhausted. Anton's mother and father found the day as hard as expected and have gone to bed. His sister cleared up and then also turned in and my family left at my request. Now I'm sitting in Anton's dressing room, holding one of his favourite tops, crying like never before. He's gone, and this is all I have left of him. Soon I will need to pack my own things and walk away from a life I loved. However, what's the point of staying anyway if he's not here?

I think I must sit hugging his top for a good hour before reluctantly I stand to go to bed. As I replace his top, I notice something shining in the corner of the shelf and reach for it carefully. It's a phone and I wonder why it's here. It's an old one, not the up to date one he had and so my curiosity gets the better of me and I sit down again and turn it on.

The phone comes to life but is password protected. The curiosity is burning me up inside because this phone is fully charged, which strikes me as odd because it means he kept it that way. Thinking of all possible passwords he could use, I finally hit on the one he used for his computer, Fleur2019, the year we met.

My heart hammers as the screen bursts into life and I start to scroll through it. I don't know why but I go immediately to the texts and register only one number. In fact, there is only one contact listed - Sunny. My heart thumps as I scroll through the texts and I feel sick at the content. These texts are disgusting and pornographic and I am disgusted when I see the lewd remarks swimming in front of my eyes. Disgusting words that must have come from someone else because this can't be Anton's phone. Whoever owns it is sick and twisted because the things they describe are surely illegal.

My hands shake as I read text after text and the bile rises in my throat as I read every word. By the time I reach the last one, I'm convinced this isn't Anton's phone. How could it be? He would never say words like this. He must have found it, or been keeping it for a friend—but who?

Then my attention turns to the photographs and I wish I never found it because as I scroll through the images, my heart breaks all over again. It's him–them–together.

Like a car crash unfolding around me, I look at every one. I play the videos and retch into the waste bin. I hear the sounds all around as I bring everything up because those images are far worse than seeing Anton lying in that pool. The face in these photographs is a familiar one and to say I'm shocked is an understatement. How did I not know about this?

Two days later

Mr Harris clears his throat and looks around the room with a grave expression, and I stare at a small piece of fluff on the carpet and prepare myself for what's about to happen.

I am sitting in the front row of a group of chairs with Anton's parents beside me. His sister and a couple of close friends are behind us and we all look at the solicitor with expectation. He has before him the last Will and Testament of Anton Richardson and I'm not expecting to be mentioned in it at all.

I was asked to attend by Mr Harris, probably because I am the resident in the house Anton owned and will probably need to sign some sort of disclaimer and move out.

He clears his throat and looks over his spectacles at us and nods respectfully.

"It is with considerable sadness that I called you all here to witness the last Will and Testament of Anton Flynn Richardson."

His mother sobs beside me and I reach out and grasp her hand in mine. I've grown to really love Anton's family and it will be hard losing them as well as him. Ever since I made my discovery on the night of the funeral, I have done my utmost to push it from my mind. I can't deal with what I saw and just need to get through the next ordeal ahead.

After reading through the preliminaries, Mr Harris comes to the main part of the Will. He reaches for an envelope on his desk and says kindly, "This letter is for you, Fleur. Anton wanted me to give this to you to read in the comfort of your own home."

I take the letter from him and my heart thumps. Anton wrote me a letter and obviously placed it with his solicitor —but why?

He clears his throat and says in a business-like voice, "Regarding the house I own in The Chase, Esher, I can confirm that it is now mortgage free and I leave it to my darling Fleur."

I hear a gasp and realise it's coming from me and I shake my head. "That can't be right."

He nods kindly. "It's true, Fleur. I drew this will up myself and it was Anton's express wish that you continue to live in the house if anything happened to him. He loved you very much, my dear."

A lone tear trickles down my face as my heart breaks all over again. He loved me. Really loved me enough to leave me his home. His mother reaches over and hugs me, saying tearfully, "I'm glad, darling. You deserve it."

His father nods and I can't help but break down in front of them and say tearfully, "I don't deserve this. It should be yours."

Mr Harris interrupts. "Anton also made provision for his family in his will."

He looks down and reads, "To my amazing parents who I owe all my success to, I leave the contents of my savings account and all my trophies and awards. Dad, I remember you always wanted one, so I leave you my beloved Ferrari. Look after her for me. I know you will."

This time, his father breaks and we all rush to comfort him in his grief.

Then, when we all contain ourselves, Mr Harris says, "To my beloved sister who used to argue with me incessantly, I leave my prized collection of sporting memorabilia and hope she gets a good price at auction. I understand you won't want to keep them because you always hated sport and told me so whenever the opportunity arose. Maybe that's why this bequest gives me the most pleasure."

Bethany nods and bows her head and Mr Harris adds, "Along with the sum of five hundred thousand pounds."

She looks up and says incredulously, "Fucking hell."

This lightens the mood, and it's strange to laugh at something so serious. Then Mr Harris peers across at Anton's mother and smiles. "To my amazing mother who I love with all my heart, please don't grieve too much mum. I know you will, but I want you to enjoy life at my expense. God knows I gave you enough cause to worry, so I'm leaving you my collection of watches to sell. They should keep you in cruises for the rest of your life and just raise a toast to me when you set sail."

It's all too much, and I pinch myself to stop the tears from falling. I am wrecked in every way and I miss him so much it physically hurts. Then Mr Harris looks back at me and says firmly, "Finally, the rest of my worldly goods and any money in my bank account go to my beloved Fleur. Now I am gone I want her to live her life like the superstar she is. I love you, babe. Never stop believing that despite what you may find."

I stiffen as I sense the questions in the air from Anton's family and vow never to reveal what I saw. They need to remember their son the way he always was, and I am not going to shatter that illusion. In fact, I haven't decided what I'm going to do with the information and pushed it aside to deal with when I'm stronger. I know one thing though; I must deal with it because this could hold the key to why he died.

CHAPTER 9

FLEUR

I bid a tearful goodbye to Anton's family and as I close the door; it strikes me that this is the first time I've been alone since the day Anton died. The house feels large, empty and soulless, and it's because all the light has gone. When I think about the will, it brings a lump to my throat. He always cared. Cared enough to leave everything to me and even more incredible is the fact his parents are happy about it. Do I deserve this, no I don't? However, I'm more determined than ever to make Anton's death count for something and so I push my grief aside and decide to solve the mystery of why he died.

My thoughts are interrupted by a gentle knock on the door and I'm surprised to find Miranda standing there, looking worried. "I'm sorry, Fleur. Please say if you'd rather be alone, but I saw Anton's parents leave and wondered if you fancied some company."

I smile sadly and beckon her inside. "Thanks, that's kind of you. Can I get you some tea?"

She nods and says softly, "If it's not too much trouble."

She follows me into the kitchen and as I busy myself with making the drinks, she says, "It must be so hard for you. I can't imagine what you're going through."

I shrug and carry on making the tea. Small talk with Miranda is not what I want right now, so I change the subject. "So, tell me, Miranda, what else has been happening around here? I could sure use the distraction right now."

I'm not sure if it's my imagination or not, but Miranda looks a little shifty. She shrugs and toys with the belt wrapped around her waist before saying, "I'm struggling, Fleur."

I stare at her sharply and she sighs. "It's James. He's always away working and when he does come home, he's overbearing and argumentative. I can't do anything right and I'm not sure what to do."

Maybe it's because I've had to deal with so much in the last few weeks. I've lost all my compassion because I sigh and say irritably, "I'm sorry, Miranda, but I have no answers for you. Perhaps you should talk to Venetia because she appears to be the only one around here with no problems."

Miranda's eyes fill and she sniffs. "I'm sorry, I don't know why, but I just can't talk to anyone like I can you. Arabella is going through so much and I know you are too, but I thought…"

"What? That I'll push aside my own problems to listen to yours. That I'll be grateful for some company because I now live alone. That I'm happy to listen to another person's problems to make my own seem not so bad. Well, for your information, I actually couldn't care less if you're having problems with James. Quite frankly, if it's that bad, leave."

Turning away, I let the anger wash over me as I deal with what I've been through and now this. Then I catch sight of Miranda's desperate face reflected back at me in the mirror and I feel bad. My shoulders sag and I say apologetically, "I'm sorry. I'm a bitch and you don't deserve a friend like me. You know, just give me a minute and I'll go and grab us a bottle of expensive wine from the cellar. God knows we both need to get wasted tonight, and it's been a long time coming. Make yourself at home. I won't be a minute."

I head off to the wine cellar that's accessed through a door in the hallway and give myself a good talking to. How could I be so hideous to Miranda, who looks as if she could badly use a friend right now? As I select a bottle of Anton's favourite wine, I sense the ever-present tears start to build and I whisper, "Don't worry, babe, I'll make everything better."

The trouble is, I'm having a lot of trouble getting my head around what I found on that phone and even more devastating was the letter Anton wrote to me. To be honest, I should blow this whole place apart with what I found out, but I can't. It's not about me, or Anton, come to mention it. No, this is bigger than both of us and I need to think long and hard about what I'm going to do because the secret I'm holding threatens to destroy lives.

Miranda and I polish off the bottle of vintage red that Anton used to love, and it feels good to let go for once. We kick off our shoes and talk long into the night. Miranda is good company, but halfway through the evening, her laughter turns to tears as the alcohol kicks in and she says sadly, "I hate my husband."

I stare at her in shock and she sniffs. "I suppose I never really loved him in the first place. It was exciting and forbidden when I first met James. He was a successful barrister, and I was a mere legal secretary and we started an affair that was carried out behind closed doors most days."

I look at her with interest and she sobs. "He's a difficult

man to live with. I suppose that comes with the job he does. At work he's God, and at home, he likes to think he is."

She takes a large slug of wine and starts to laugh hysterically. "But I have a secret, Fleur."

My ears prick up and I hold my breath as she slurs, "Oh yes, my very own secret. If James ever found out, it would abso-bloody-lutely destroy the bastard. He thinks he's so clever and controlling. Does that surprise you, Fleur? James likes to control, and I'm no exception. He's a skinflint and a miser and he won't give me a penny more than is necessary because he's a bloody miserable, tight bastard."

She drinks the rest of the wine as if it's a glass of water and hiccups loudly. "Oops, sorry."

I notice the tears building behind her eyes and regard a woman on the edge before me. I may be in a living hell, but it appears I'm not the only one. What with Arabella, myself and now it appears Miranda, I wonder what Desdemona Fortune saw that day.

Out of sheer curiosity, I say quickly, "What did that fortune teller say to you, Miranda?"

The fear fill her eyes and she whispers, "Trouble. Big, bad, trouble and pain. That's what she told me. She told me I was facing a challenge I may not overcome. I'm not going to lie. It scared me, Fleur. What do you think she meant?"

Shaking my head, I say flippantly, "You'll get pregnant and it will hurt."

Her eyes widen and then she starts laughing hysterically. "That's funny. I thought you had to actually have sex to get pregnant. If I am, it will be the second coming because James and I haven't been near each other for years."

She sets down her glass and staggers towards the door. "I won't be long; I just need the ladies."

I watch her go and wonder how a woman can become so drunk on what appears to be two glasses of wine. She's either a total lightweight, or has been stocking up the alcohol in her system before she arrived?

My head starts to hurt as the walls close in on me and I crave some fresh air. I need to get away and the more I think of it, the more my mind's made up. First thing tomorrow, I'm getting the hell out of here and I know just where I'm going.

PART III

MIRANDA

CHAPTER 1

MIRANDA

I hear the door slam and wait for the car to start. Today may prove to be a good day. I've had to put my little hobby on hold for the last few weeks due to the problems close to home. The place has been awash with reporters and film crews, all anxious to get the big scoop on Anton.

As I think of the poor man, the tears well up in my eyes. He was so lovely, so beautiful and now he's so dead. Poor Fleur. She loved him so much and now he's gone.

Why do the good always die young and leave the miserable old bastards behind to irritate the rest of us?

I see James staring pompously out of the painting he had done of himself in his robes and I stick my tongue out. Then I run to my dressing room and reach for the top shelf and the source of all my delight. My treasure.

I open the lid reverently and stare inside, my mouth watering in anticipation. Then I lift out the beautiful brooch with a diamond centre, surrounded by rubies. It flashes as the sunlight catches it and makes my heart sing. Perfect.

I can actually remember James's mother wearing this. She

wore it all the time, and it was one of her most prized possessions. When she died last year, James inherited all her jewellery and because of the nature of the man, he has had it all locked away in his safe ever since. However, there isn't as much there as before because I have been, shall we say, borrowing pieces for months now. I get them duplicated by a contact I made at a fair I attended and they are made into exact copies. I always tell the same story. I don't want to risk getting my jewellery stolen or damaged, but want to wear the pieces. The copies are made for my own pleasure and that's achieved when I take them to the pawnshop and exchange them for hard cash. The copy goes back in the safe and the stupid old fool is none the wiser. Then I get to spend the money on frivolous piffery and enjoy telling James it cost next to nothing in the charity shop.

Giggling to myself, I wrap the brooch in my handkerchief and place it carefully in my bag. A trip to town is necessary today, and that makes me happy when there is very little else to be happy about.

Two hours later and I'm standing in my usual pawn shop looking at Jake greedily. "Hmm, nice piece, Arabella. Where did you say this was from?"

I smile and adjust the black wig I'm wearing, covered with a Louis Vuitton headscarf. "My mother, darling. She left it to me when she passed, poor love. It pains me to part with it, but you know how hard times are."

Jake nods and I realise he couldn't care less where this is from. All he wants is a profit and I expect that most of the jewellery I sell him goes to auction, not sit alongside the various cameras and gold chains that sit proudly on the surrounding shelves.

I watch him count out five hundred pounds and my heart flutters. Five hundred pounds for a piece of James's family history. If he knew, it would send him to an early grave which almost tempts me into telling him—almost.

I spend the afternoon shopping on Bond Street. The brooch wasn't the only thing I sold, and I knew today would be a good day. Two thousand pounds worth of shopping later, I head home. Yes, retail therapy is the answer to all life's problems and I'm so glad I found a way out of mine.

* * *

James shouts for me as soon as he steps foot inside the door. "Miranda, bring my coffee to my study. I have work to do."

Sighing, I set about making the coffee like the dutiful little wife I am and wonder how it came to this. James and I used to be in love, but our flame burned out years ago. Now I resort to reading racy novels and pleasuring myself, rather than subject myself to him heaving himself on and off me at the end of a trying day. We have even resorted to separate rooms because it was easier than listening to him snoring. He was happy about the arrangement, which makes me realise he hates me just as much as I do him.

"Miranda, where's that bloody coffee?"

Gritting my teeth, I go in search of him and say brightly, "Sorry, here it is."

He grunts and I notice the briefcase overflowing with papers and say briskly, "Dinner will be ready in one hour. Will you be eating with me, or would you like a tray?"

He waves me away. "Of course I'll eat with you. Until then, I don't want to be disturbed."

Sighing, I close the door behind me and walk back to the kitchen. To be honest, I'm always happier when he locks himself away in his study for hours on end because it means I'm off the hook.

The phone rings and I pounce on it, just hoping for some

good conversation. My life is a little lonely and I've even been known to talk to cold callers for ages just for something to do. However, today it's Venetia. "Hey, Miranda, how are things?"

"Ok, what about you?"

She sighs heavily. "Matthew's away and I'm bored. Arabella and Fleur are obviously tied up with more problems than a person should stand, and I'm at a loose end. Do you fancy heading out for a drink somewhere nice?"

I'm excited at the thought of getting away from James for the night and say eagerly, "Great, what time?"

"I'll pick you up at eight if that's ok."

"Perfect. Thanks, Venetia, I owe you one."

I replace the receiver and quickly hurry the dinner along. This is a great opportunity to wear that new Chloe dress I bought today. Hopefully, we'll end up somewhere good, because I love nothing more than flirting with a total stranger while James sits festering at home.

As soon as dinner is ready, I call him and he sits down heavily on the chair opposite before flicking on the news. There is no conversation which suits me fine because I have nothing to say to him.

As I watch him eat, it strikes me that I don't even know him anymore. I don't ask how his job is going, what he does of an evening locked in his study and who his friends even are? As we finish up, I say brightly, "I'm heading out with Venetia tonight. I'm not sure what time I'll be home."

He looks up with interest. "Since when?"

"Since an hour ago when she called and asked me. You don't mind, do you?"

He shakes his head. "No, why would I? Remember it's the end of the month. Do you have enough housekeeping left for this?"

I snap irritably, "Yes."

He looks thoughtful. "Hmm, I figured I was overly

generous last month. Maybe we could cut back a little next month."

Rolling my eyes, I say angrily, "Are you saying we can't afford it?"

He looks annoyed. "Of course not. We have more than enough money."

"Then why do you ration it out so much? For goodness' sake, James, I sometimes feel as if we live on the breadline. I'm pretty sure you'd send me off to the local food bank if you thought you could get away with it."

"Don't be facetious, Miranda, it doesn't suit you. You know why I'm careful and there is a very good example of it over the road. What would happen if I lost my job like Anthony? You don't work, so it all falls to me. I'm being careful for our future and you can complain all you like, but you know it makes sense."

The exasperation grabs hold of my better judgement and shout, "You're so hell-bent on saving for our future, James. You have appeared to overlook the fact we may not have one if you continue shutting me out like this."

There's an awkward silence as I voice something that has been festering for months now. Then he says in a shocked voice, "What are you saying?"

"I don't know, James. Can't you see what's happening? Where has it all gone wrong?"

"Wrong?"

"Yes, wrong," I say wearily. "We used to be a couple and were two people in love who actually wanted to be together. When did that change into this? Separate rooms, vicious words and secrets."

He looks at me sharply and I immediately regret my choice of words. "Secrets? Do you care to explain what you mean by that?"

Sighing with exasperation, I start clearing away the dishes

and practically yell. "No, I do not care to explain! Look at us, we're hardly middle-aged and yet we live as if we are. This house is crammed full of things that old people cherish, not people our age. You act as if you're drawing your pension, but you're still young. Do you hear that James, you are still young and we should be enjoying our lives, not waiting to die?"

He looks so shocked; I start laughing hysterically, and his eyes narrow. "Have you been drinking again?"

This makes me laugh even harder, and he flings down his serviette and storms out, shouting, "I don't know who you are anymore?"

Laughing, I shout after him. "Because you bloody well never spend any time with me, so it's no wonder I'm a stranger to you, James."

The door slamming is all the answer I get and I look around me with anger.

Staring at the dirty dishes in the sink, I turn my back on them and head for the stairs and my own little corner of paradise - my dressing room, where I can pretend I am someone else entirely. I have many alter egos and it's no wonder. Tonight, I must be plain old boring Miranda Donnelly, but I've been known to be many different women. Sometimes I head out to lunch as someone else completely and relish the attentions of smart men who are desperate for a date. Yes, Miranda Donnelly has a secret and not just one either. She enjoys dates with men she meets off the Internet because it's thrilling and adventurous and she can be anyone she wants to be except the person she hates the most —herself.

CHAPTER 2

MIRANDA

"*Hi*, Venetia. You're looking lovely."

Venetia smiles, and I wasn't lying because tonight she does. She's wearing a beautiful emerald green dress that complements her amazing red hair, which is hanging long and wavy down her back. Her fair skin looks glowing and, on the whole, she looks totally amazing.

She smiles with gratitude and says in her trademark husky voice, "I went to a spa for a few days. It was just what the doctor ordered after the emotions of the last few weeks."

I stare at her in surprise because, out of all us, Venetia appears to have no emotion. She's always been the closed one of the group. There's a wall she puts up that lets hardly anyone in and she can be totally relied upon to be level-headed and the one who always tells it how it is.

As I stare at her, it strikes me that I don't really know much about her at all. Mind you, if my friends knew half the stuff about me, they would be astonished.

She drives towards the town and says unexpectedly, "Have you seen much of Arabella lately?"

"Not really. Her parents came, and I wasn't brave enough to go and call. I know Fleur did and there was some sort of altercation, but that all happened before... well, Anton."

Venetia nods. "Terrible business. I still can't believe he's gone, can you? Poor Fleur."

"Yes, poor Fleur. I know we all doubted her sincerity when she first came, but I really do believe she loved Anton."

Nodding, Venetia says sadly, "I wonder what she'll do now?"

Thinking back to our conversation yesterday, I say sadly, "She's struggling. She was quite cold towards me when I popped round and I heard she's going away for a few days."

"Do you know where?"

"No, but probably to stay with one of her friends from Anton's club. We forget she's part of another crowd sometimes and they will know more than most what she's going through."

"Why, have their husbands been murdered too?"

I stare at Venetia in surprise, because her sharp tone is unexpected. "No... I didn't mean that... of course not."

She sighs. "I'm sorry. I don't know why I'm so on edge. What happened to Anton is truly terrible and, of course, not normal. Perhaps I'm just on edge about this whole thing. If Anton was murdered, then who did it? This place is like a fortress most of the time and if anyone got in, surely one of us would have seen them. Just getting past those electric gates is a feat in itself, then again... you don't think that it could have been..."

I shake my head in horror. "One of us? Oh my god, Venetia, no, of course, it wouldn't be any of us. We loved Anton. Why would any of us kill him?"

She shrugs. "Perhaps it was an accident. Who knows, he may have been arguing with someone; the bruises on his body would explain a fight. Maybe he was pushed and hit his head."

"I doubt it. If that did happen, whoever he argued with would have pulled him out and called for help. No, I don't think it was murder, or an argument. Probably he was walking by his pool and slipped and his injuries were a result of that."

Venetia laughs softly. "Typical Miranda, always looking for the good in everyone and the simplest explanation. What does James think? He's seen a few cases in his time. Surely he has an opinion on this?"

My heart twists at the mention of James and I say bitterly, "I wouldn't know."

Venetia looks at me with interest as I sigh heavily. "We don't talk anymore. James and I, well... we may live in the same house, but we lead very separate lives. I'm not sure when it all happened, but has been the case for some time now."

To my surprise, Venetia nods. "Same."

I stare at her in shock and she laughs dully. "Matthew and I are like ships in the night. I work away a lot and when I'm home, he works. We haven't had a holiday in ages and our sex life is practically non-existent."

She turns into a parking bay outside the local wine bar and says with determination. "Come on, let's go and have some fun. I don't know about you, but I need to switch off from The Chase and all its problems for one night. How about we forget our partners, enjoy a few drinks and remember the women we are for once?"

As I follow her inside, I say quickly, "What about the car? You can't drink."

She shrugs. "Then we'll get a cab home, or who knows, perhaps some kind man will offer us a lift? Come on,

Miranda, let's forget our stuffy husbands for one night and remind ourselves that we're attractive women who deserve better."

As I follow her inside, it strikes me how little I know of my friend. I never thought for one moment she was going through the same thing as I am and it makes my heart lift a little. Yes, I'm up for a spot of serious flirting tonight because increasingly I'm becoming aware that my marriage is on the rocks and I need to find a replacement- sharpish.

* * *

The wine bar is heaving tonight and by the time we grab a bottle of Prosecco, it's quite difficult to find a seat. Luckily, we notice a couple getting ready to leave in the centre of the room and quickly take their place.

Conversation is difficult because the noise is off the scale, so I just glance around me with interest and soon a man sitting opposite catches my eye. He is looking at me with a thoughtful expression and I smile before turning away. Hm, just my type. Dark hair, rough beard and clothes that tell me he takes care of himself.

Feeling conscious of him, I smile and act like a woman with no cares or worries. I pout suggestively and laugh at the conversation and just feel glad that I no longer wear my wedding ring. James hasn't even noticed, but I stopped wearing it weeks ago. It now lives in my jewellery box because I can no longer stand the sight of it. It chains me to a loveless marriage and I want out.

Venetia appears to be on some sort of mission herself, and I recognise the lost expression in her eyes as she downs several glasses of Prosecco and desperately tries to enjoy herself. There's a sadness to her that reaches out and pulls me in, because I must wear that same expression on my face. I'm surprised, though, because Matthew is a sweetheart. He's always been funny, sweet and a bit of a joker. I've always envied Venetia because he appears to idolise her. In a crowded room, he always searched for her with his eyes. I see the longing mixed with pride when he watches her, and I always considered them the dream couple. The standard we all hoped to reach one day and yet here she is, looking so sad, it makes me catch my breath.

It must be an hour later that she says loudly, "All of that Prosecco has made me need the ladies. I won't be long."

Nodding, I watch her scrape back her chair and leave, and I turn my attention to my glass instead. However, almost as soon as she's gone, her chair is taken and I stare in surprise as the man from across the bar slides into her seat and looks at me with so much heat in his gaze I'm blown away.

"Hi, I'm Miles Sullivan. I hope you don't mind, but I've been watching you for some time now and you intrigue me."

I blush. "Me?"

He nods and leans in and I swallow hard. "Yes, you. Tell me, what brings you out drinking on a Wednesday night?"

"Why not? My friend asked, and I fancied the company. I could say the same thing to you."

He smiles and my pulse starts to race as my gaze travels the length of him. He has that confident aura of a man who knows he wants. A tanned chest peeks out from a shirt unbuttoned low enough to provide a glimpse of a hard chest, with a smattering of dark hair. A rough stubble-filled face gives him a masculine edge and his dark brown eyes flash as he devours me with one long, sexy look. I feel my mouth dry and run my tongue over my lips, my heart beating frantically as I imagine all sorts of deprivation at his hands.

This man is every naughty dream I've ever had, and he is looking at me with such intent that it takes my breath away.

Leaning in, he says in a husky voice, "I would like to get to know you better, but time is against us."

I gasp, "Why?"

My heart flutters as he says ruefully, "Because I leave for New York in the morning."

"Forever?"

He nods. "I run a business out there and will be away for some time. The trouble is, now I've met you and it kind of changes everything."

"Why?"

"Because you are everything I've been looking for and I've been looking for a long time."

My head starts spinning as the power of his words hits me. I try to tell myself he's just spinning me a tale, a pickup line that he must use every day but he's hit the jackpot with me because I'm desperate, needy and so open to adventure, I could write a book on it.

I note Venetia heading my way and he says urgently, "Meet me outside in five minutes."

I feel my heart thumping as he leaves and Venetia says in surprise, "Who was that?"

I laugh nervously and reach for the bottle, pouring myself a large glass. "Some man trying his luck."

Looking after him, Venetia whistles. "He's impressive. What did you say?"

I shrug as if indifferent. "Nothing. I am married, after all."

Venetia laughs. "But your marriage ended ages ago, as did mine."

I stare at her in surprise. "What are you saying?"

Suddenly, she looks so sad it takes my breath away. "I'm saying I've made mistakes, and the biggest one was marrying Matthew. He's a decent guy, but he bores me to death. He's everything I'm not and living with him is suffocating me. I go away a lot to escape him and I don't know what to do about it."

She holds up the empty bottle of Prosecco and smiles

sadly. "I'm getting us another one of these. I need alcohol tonight to dull the pain."

As she makes to leave, I say quickly, "I'll just head to the ladies. I won't be long."

She nods and I quickly head outside before I change my mind. This should be interesting.

CHAPTER 3

MIRANDA

I almost back out, but then the image of James sitting surrounded by his case notes in the study spurs me on. He's so bloody old these days and I'm still young and vivacious. I want a bit of danger in my life and this man made me feel more alive in one minute than James has in months.

Before my head wins and sends me back to my seat, I step outside and hear, "I'm glad you came."

Spinning around, I see Miles leaning against the wall and my mouth waters. Out here in the cool night with the steady thump of life going on inside the bar, I experience the thrill of excitement at the unknown. He moves to the shadows and says darkly, "Come over here."

My heart flutters as I do what I've always been told not to and move towards the stranger as if he has me on an invisible line and is reeling me in.

As I step into the shadows with him, my heart starts racing as our fingers meet and he pulls me close. No words are spoken as our lips crash together and he plunders my mouth with his tongue. His stubble grazes my chin and sends me wild and I arch against him, just desperate for a hard body against mine.

He pushes me back against the wall and presses into me, and I love every second of it. This is wild and unscripted, and I love it. Tonight, I am not Miranda Donnelly. I am a scarlet woman having a liaison with a handsome stranger. This is the stuff of movies and I'm the leading lady. I don't even think about the danger involved. I'm too far gone for that and I push his shirt up and relish the touch of his soft skin under my fingers as I let my hands roam freely all over him. But it isn't enough.

I'm conscious that his hands have started wandering and as he presses into me, I feel his interest hard against me and it makes me believe I'm so attractive, so wanted and so sexy. It's like a drug. He pushes my dress around my waist and I gasp with pleasure as I fumble with his belt and unfasten his trousers. Then I do something I've never done in my life; I have sex with a stranger up against the wall in a dark alley behind a bar, and it's astonishingly amazing.

Not ten minutes later, I walk back into the bar feeling hot, dirty and used. As soon as we finished, Miles tucked his business card into my bra and whispered, "I must go, but I want to see you again. Take my card and call me when you can get away. I'll arrange a flight for you to New York and we can explore each other more leisurely next time."

I watched him walk away towards a Lamborghini parked outside and my mind is well and truly messed up. Miles is my dream man and what just happened was fate.

As I take my seat again, Venetia looks at me thoughtfully. "You were ages."

Reaching for another glass of Prosecco, I wink. "Not really, it was quite quick, really."

Venetia's expression makes me giggle as she notes my flushed cheeks and messed up hair. She surely must notice that my lipstick is smeared, and she shakes her head slowly, "You lucky cow."

We giggle as we raise a glass to each other and I say, "To the rest of our lives, Venetia."

As the glasses touch, I see a determination in my friend's eyes that matches my own. Yes, we may be chained to men we no longer love, but ultimately, we have the control. It's now up to both of us to make our futures bright and as I feel the little piece of hope nestling against my breast, I make up my mind. I will call Miles and I will go to New York. I just need a few more visits to the pawnshop to make it happen.

* * *

The next day after I drop Venetia back to the wine bar to retrieve her car, I do what I've been itching to do all night. Head into town. I contain my usual disguise in my bag because I'm not stupid enough to pawn items under my own name. No, I quite like the fact I dress as my neighbours and Arabella has become a firm favourite with me. It was easier to adopt the persona of people I knew and Arabella pawns stuff, which is quite ironic when you think of her current situation. Fleur often goes out on dates with my Internet friends and Venetia is quite often seen buying clothes and shoes on Bond Street. I love escaping Miranda Donnelly whenever I can because that woman bores me rigid. It's much more exciting being my cool friends and so, it's with confidence, I head towards Jake's shop.

As I reach it, there is a little nagging doubt in my mind that I've gone too far this time. The item I've brought with me isn't the usual jewellery. This time it's something that was totally out of character and proves how desperate I've become—Anton's Rolex.

My heart starts racing faster as I remember seeing it on the hall table when I visited Fleur not long after it all happened. She was in such a state I'm doubtful if she even knew what day it was and seeing the watch on the side was like a red rag to a bull. Before I could even question my judgement and morality, I put it into my pocket and have been wrestling with my conscience ever since.

I mean, it's hardly likely it will be missed. There is no engraving to differentiate it from any other. Anton will never search for it and it is doubtful Fleur even knows it's missing. No, this was a gift from God and I took it. Gold Rolex's cost an absolute fortune, which is why I need to sell it today. I spent all night re-living my encounter with Miles and as soon as I can, I am calling him to carry on where we left off.

"Morning Arabella."

I smile as I see Jake greeting me from behind his usual counter. "What have you got for me today?"

I smile and remove the watch carefully. "Something quite valuable, actually, Jake. Today I need some money to take a trip and this one will do the job perfectly."

As he sees the expensive item, his eyes widen and the greed fills them. Yes, Anton's watch will do us both nicely and any guilt I have is pushed firmly to the side because who will this hurt, anyway?

When I leave the pawnshop, it's as if I've won on the scratch cards. Ten thousand pounds! Who knew it would be worth that much? I'm under no illusions that it's worth probably triple that because Jake is a shrewd operator and, from the expression in his eyes, we both hit the jackpot with this one.

My heart thumps as I leave the store with the cash burning a hole in my handbag. That was so easy and any guilt I may have had deserted me the moment I lay my hands on those crisp notes. I am elated, euphoric and so turned on I don't even recognise myself.

Before I can change my mind, I reach for my phone and

dial Mile's number and hold my breath as it rings. A sleepy voice answers, "Miles Sullivan."

Just the sound of the gravelly voice laced with sleep turns me on and I say softly, "Hi, Miles. It's Miranda from the wine bar."

A low chuckle crosses the airwaves and he says sexily, "My dangerous liaison. I've been dreaming of you. In fact, I'm picturing you beside me right now."

The desire hits me as I say huskily, "Do you fancy some company?"

He laughs. "Sure. When were you thinking?"

"How about next week?"

There's a short silence and then he says huskily, "I'll arrange a flight for you and a car to collect you from the airport. Text me your details and honey, I'll be planning your trip myself. The things you'll experience will make you never want to leave."

My head starts spinning as I picture the sexy man lying in bed thousands of miles away and I say softly, "I'll hold you to that."

I hang up and am giddy at the thought of what just happened. I have enough money and now a plan. I just need to invent a reason to escape for a week and I'm all set. New York, here I come.

CHAPTER 4

MIRANDA

*O*nce James is out of the way, I start deciding what I'm going to take with me to New York. I texted Miles my details, and he sent me the flight details in return. Now all I need to do is pack and tell James I'm heading off for a week and all is good.

As I'm pacing, the front doorbell rings and I'm annoyed. Bother, I really wanted the time to get everything organised today and now this will set me back.

However, my face lights up when I see Arabella standing outside and I say happily, "Hey, do you fancy a coffee?"

She nods gratefully and follows me inside and I say lightly, "I haven't seen you for ages. How's the job going?"

"Great. I never envisioned I'd enjoy it as much as I do. The people are amazing and I've settled in really well."

I hand her the coffee and say with envy. "At least you have a purpose. I'm chained to the kitchen sink most days."

Arabella nods because she knows only too well what it's like caring for a husband who foots all the bills. "Why don't you get a job then?"

"Perhaps I should. To be honest, I need something

because life is getting stale. James is always working and even when he is here, he's shut away in his study doing more work, probably. I've tried to get him to relax, but he's so far gone he's a lost cause."

Arabella nods. "Anthony has always been a bit like that. He has always worked hard, but when he came home, I was always his top priority. The trouble is, ever since it all went wrong, he's been so cold and acting as if it's all my fault."

"Your fault! How did he work that one out?"

"I'm not sure. Even my new job appeared to anger him. He even invited my parents who I can't stand and spent more time with them than me. I'm at a loss as to what I've done wrong and now he won't even speak to me."

I stare at her in surprise because it's common knowledge that Arabella was always the luckiest one of us. A good-looking husband who was successful and famous. Classic good looks and an effortless style. More money than most and an exquisite home, bang up to date and on-trend. I always envied Arabella, we all did and now that has changed for the worse.

I smile sympathetically and say, "How is Anthony? Is there any news on his operation?"

"No, but then again, how would I know? He never talks to me and is just plain rude when I try. Then there's that hotel invoice I found. It's made me mistrustful and I've been rifling through his pockets at every opportunity, hoping to find some sort of evidence. To be honest, Miranda, I'm at my wit's end and now Fleur's away I have no one to turn to."

I grab her hand and say warmly, "You've got me and Venetia, so why don't we all get together and get everything off our chests? Venetia and I went drinking the other night, and it was the best night I've had in ages."

I feel bad when Arabella looks a little put out and says shortly, "Why wasn't I invited?"

I'm a little embarrassed because it's common knowledge she doesn't have any money now but that aside, we should have invited her. Some friends we turned out to be and I say apologetically, "I'm sorry, we didn't think."

Shrugging, she looks around and says kindly, "Your house is always so interesting, Miranda."

It makes me want to laugh because if she had said dull and interesting, that would have been a better description. "It's James's taste, not mine. He likes the old school look whereas I much prefer yours and Fleurs. Even Venetia's home is more up to date than mine, and she hardly spends any money on it."

Arabella nods. "Yes, I've always wondered why. It's very sparsely furnished, almost as if they can't agree on a theme."

I laugh. "They probably can't and from what she told me the other night; they can't agree on anything."

Arabella looks shocked and I say sadly, "Yes, Venetia and Matthew are struggling in much the same way as the rest of us. Only Fleur has a different set of problems. Do you know how she is, by the way?"

"She called last night and told me she was staying for another week. She asked me to water the plants, which I am glad to do."

"Where is she staying?"

She shrugs. "I don't know. All she said was that it was an old friend. She probably needed to clear her head and create some distance from the situation. It must be hard living in that huge house with all the memories of Anton everywhere."

I nod, a little uncomfortable at the mention of Anton. Now I've done it, I feel terrible at stealing his watch and wonder if I should try to buy it back. I've still got a few weeks before Jake sells it. Hearing Arabella express so much concern and sympathy for our friend makes me feel like a terrible human being, so I decide immediately to go and buy

back the watch. I'll have to sell something in the safe to raise
the money – but what?

Then an idea forms in my mind and like a fungus, it starts
to spread and grow. That's it, the solution to everything.
Why didn't I think of it before – its pure genius.

I almost can't wait for Arabella to leave so I can plan it all
out. This could be the end for James and me and the beginning of something amazing with Miles. What I have planned
will set me free and pay back Fleur for what I stole. Brilliant.

CHAPTER 5

MIRANDA

*T*he next few days are probably the most frustrating of my life. James is working from home and I can't put my plan into action. It annoys me because he is so rarely at home and the one time I do need him gone, he's here.

After about the tenth coffee I delivered to his study, I snap. "Why are you here, James?"

He looks surprised. "Um, I live here."

"Well, obviously, but why aren't you at the office? Have you lost your job like Anthony and can't bring yourself to tell me?"

He looks angry and says roughly, "You're a bitch sometimes, Miranda. How could you say something like that when poor Anthony is struggling?"

I laugh. "Aren't we all, darling?"

Sighing, he nods to the seat in front of him and I'm a little worried. Goodness, this is unusual. James actually wants to talk, which is news in itself.

He leans back in his chair and sighs heavily.

"I've got some news and you need to sit down."

I feel anxious because, from the expression in his eyes, it's not good news.

He says somewhat guiltily, "I've been struggling, Miranda. Mentally, emotionally and physically."

I hold my breath as he says sadly, "I've been drinking - a lot. It's why I spend so much time in here, so I can drink without you seeing me. By the time I drag myself to bed, you are fast asleep and none the wiser."

I gasp, "But why, James?"

"Because I'm weak. Because I can't cope and everything got on top of me. The bad news is, I've been caught driving under the influence and I'm due in court next week."

I stare at him in total surprise. "Next week!"

He nods. "I was clocked doing one hundred mph on the A3. I stand to lose my licence and could go to prison."

I feel light-headed and stutter, "Prison, surely not!"

He shakes his head and reaches for the coffee, saying sadly, "I hope it won't come to that. I've got a good friend of mine pleading my case and he's confident I'll just get a ban and a fine. It may make the news though, so you should be warned."

My mind is racing away with me as I struggle to digest his words. Then it hits me, "But I'm away next week."

He looks surprised. "Since when?"

The lies start spilling from my lips as I say quickly, "An old school friend who's moved to New York and asked me to go and stay. She's sent the ticket and everything; I can't possibly let her down."

James looks shocked. "Who is this school friend? You never mentioned her?"

I shake my head. "Probably because we don't talk anymore. You know, James, I really need this trip because I've been so lonely. You're never here and it's as if we've grown apart. We don't even sleep in the same room and I'm at my wit's end. When the invitation came, I sort of pounced on it because I need that time away to get my head straight."

I know I'm babbling, but I'd say anything to get on that plane and looking at James's face, he believes every word I say. Nodding, he smiles sweetly. "I'm sorry, darling, I never thought about how you were feeling. I suppose I've been so wrapped up in my own problems, I never considered them rubbing off on us—our marriage. Maybe this has been a good thing. It could bring us closer and, who knows, we may even learn to laugh again?"

I register the sadness in his eyes and it brings a lump to my throat. He's right. We never took the time to talk and I know in my heart it's now too late. I feel bad for the drinking and the court case, but I'm so selfish I can't see past my own desires and want nothing to come between me and my trip to visit Miles.

Reaching across the desk, I take his hand in mine and say gently, "As soon as I get back, we'll talk. I mean, really talk. Maybe you're right and we can start again and re-discover the people we were who fell in love. I certainly hope so, and perhaps this trip will do us both the power of good."

He squeezes my hand and smiles. "You go. You're right, you need this trip. Make sure you have fun and don't worry about a thing. I'm pretty confident this mess will be sorted by the time you get home and then we'll talk."

Smiling, the relief accompanies me to the door. As I place my hand on the handle, he calls out, "Oh and Miranda…"

I turn and he says in surprise, "Where's your wedding ring?"

I peer down and laugh nervously. "Upstairs, darling. I took it off to wash my hair earlier and forgot to put it back on."

He nods, seemingly satisfied with my response and says, "Remember to put it back on. I like to see that you're mine."

My heart thumps as I walk away from him. His. He has got to be joking. I'm not his and probably never was. Everything I just said was done to buy me some time because despite what I said, I can't get away from him quickly enough.

The morning of my trip comes and to say I'm excited is an understatement. I've packed carefully and have the necessary documents via the App on my phone. I'm excited that Miles has booked me a first-class ticket and I wonder about him. He certainly appeared to have money judging by the car he drove away in, but other than that, I know nothing at all about him. This is the most reckless thing I've ever done in my life and I'm intoxicated by the whole situation. I know I'm being selfish and disloyal but for some reason, I've convinced myself it's ok. My marriage is on the rocks and I'm moving on and the money I've acquired from selling things was half mine, anyway.

As usual, James has kept his distance and seconded himself in his study most evenings, which suits me fine. It's given me ample time to prepare for this trip and what needs doing beforehand.

My heart flutters when I think of what I have planned. I've almost convinced myself it's a bad idea and that I should quit while I'm ahead, but maybe it's the danger of the whole situation that's giving me the desire to see this through.

I wake around five am on the morning of my trip and make a big fuss of getting ready. Just before I leave, James emerges from the spare bedroom bleary-eyed and I can tell he was up drinking late last night, judging by the red-rimmed eyes and vacant expression on his face.

He runs his fingers through his hair and says in a tired voice, "You're off then."

Nodding, I reach up and peck him on the cheek, saying

cheerily, "I'll be back in a week. I hope the court case goes well, darling. I'll be thinking of you."

He nods. "Thanks, I'm sure it'll be fine and it's probably a good thing you're out of the way of it all."

Smiling, I head towards the door and grab my suitcases and carry-on bag. As I make to leave, James says suddenly, "I'm sorry, Miranda."

"For what?"

The expression on his face stops me in my tracks, as he says with emotion, "For everything."

I watch as he turns away and heads back to the spare bedroom and a little part of me feels incredibly sad that this is what we've become. Strangers living in the same house but journeying down different paths. I never knew this would be our future and wonder when it all started to go so badly wrong.

However, now is not the time to worry about my marriage because I have lots to do before my flight this afternoon.

After placing my luggage in my car, I pull out of the driveway and head for the local park because I need somewhere to hide out for a while until I know the coast is clear.

CHAPTER 6

MIRANDA

*N*ine thirty comes quickly and I don't have long. I head back to The Chase and hope that everyone has left as usual. James will have left by seven to catch the train to London. Arabella leaves just before nine to be at the country club by nine thirty. Anthony is always at work, it seems, and Matthew always leaves at seven thirty on the dot. Fleur is still away and Venetia is on a trip. Perfect.

As I drive through the electric gates, my heart thumps and I feel the adrenalin kick in. I pull up on our drive and head back through the front door and call out, "James, are you home?"

The silence greets me and I smile to myself. I pull on my gloves, then I head to his study and quickly open the safe, removing all the carefully placed contents and scatter the papers around the room. I put the items in a bag and then make sure to open the drawers and spill the contents to the ground. Anything of value in my sight, I add to the rest in the bag and then look about me with relief.

Job done.

I move through the house and ransack drawers and

remove any valuables until I have quite a haul. Then I head to the back door and carefully unlock it, but leave the key in its place. Next, I smash the window above the lock with the torch we keep in the cupboard and relish the sound of breaking glass all around.

If I have any guilt about burgling my own home, it's well hidden. All I feel is euphoria because this way I get to sell the valuables and James never finds out that I replaced his mother's jewellery in the first place. I'll then have enough money to buy back the Rolex, which I put back in Fleur's home at the earliest available opportunity. James gets the insurance money, and no harm is done. I'm a genius.

I head back to my car and carefully lock the front door behind me and as I drive away from The Chase, I congratulate myself on a well-executed plan. Now I just need to stop at my usual pawnshop and recover the Rolex, and then it will be straight to the airport to begin an adventure that promises so much pleasure.

PART IV

VENETIA

CHAPTER 1

VENETIA

*a*s I make the drive home, I feel sick. Sick of my life, sick of what I've become and sick of pretending. I'm not sure how my life spiralled out of control as quickly as it did, but I was powerless to stop it.

The phone rings and I answer it on hand-free. "Hey, babe."

"Hey, just checking you arrived back safely."

I experience a twinge of guilt as I say lightly, "Yes, no problem. I'm tired though."

"I'm not surprised. Why don't you grab some sleep? I'll be home around seven and we can eat out if you prefer?"

My eyes fill with the ever-present tears and once again I'm reminded of how lucky I am. Matthew is the husband of dreams and I'm the wife of nightmares.

I swallow hard and say gratefully, "Sounds great, thanks."

His voice softens, and he says in a whisper, "I love you."

The words sound false to my own ears as I say, "Me too. See you later."

I cut the call quickly before he says anything else and the waves of nausea wash over me. Not now, Oh God, not again.

Pulling up by the side of the road, I sprint from the car and empty my stomach on the grass verge. I can't stop heaving and as my legs shake, the tears roll down my face as I face the fact I've been trying to deny for the last few weeks—I'm pregnant.

I take some deep breaths of air and reach for a tissue in my pocket to wipe away the bile resting on my lips. Pregnant. How could I be so stupid? I don't want children; I never did and now one careless act has left me with a life sentence. I lean against the car and try to control my breathing, but it's hard. I lost control of everything months ago and went down a road I should have avoided like the plague.

I wait for the dizzy feeling to subside and then climb back inside the car and as I set off for home, I think about my options. I could have a termination and then nobody would ever know. I could carry on with the pregnancy and just be happy that I've brought another life into the world, or I could face the consequences and confess everything.

As I think about my problem, that visit to the fortune-teller comes to mind and her words hit me hard all over again. "You have no future."

What does that even mean? Of course, I have a future and it's up to me to shape it into the one I want it to be.

As I park on my driveway, I look across at my neighbour's house and my stomach twists. Anthony and Arabella. They have it all, or they did until Anthony dropped his bombshell a few weeks ago. It was unexpected and shocking and it took me some time to understand what it all means because their life is about to change for good and it's all his fault.

He gambled away their future and has now paid the price, but Arabella stood by her man and proven to be the good little wife she always was. My eyes narrow as I look at the house I want above all others. The tasteful furnishings, the dressing room filled with designer clothes and, most of all, her husband.

Looking down at my stomach, I rest my hand there and smile. Yes, I want her husband because my baby needs its father. I wanted to be Arabella so much I started something that quickly escalated and now I am the one with something she wants more than anything—Anthony's baby.

As I let myself indoors, I reach for my phone again and dial the number I call above all others. He answers on the first ring and says huskily, "Missing me already?"

I laugh softly. "Of course. I just wanted to say thank you for such an amazing few days. I do love you."

"I love you too. The bed is lonely without you in it."

I have a warm feeling inside and say softly, "I wish we could be together all the time."

There's a short silence before he says gently, "You know I want that above everything, but we need to pick our moment. I can't risk Arabella finding out about us while things are so up in the air."

I laugh softly. "I thought you did a good job of stalling her with the cancer story."

He laughs. "Yes, thanks for the tip-off. The last thing I need right now is a hysterical wife to deal with. It was a good plan that may have bought us some time."

Not for the first time of asking I sigh heavily. "When is the right time, Anthony? I want you; you want me and both our marriages are over. When can we come clean and own up? I understand things are uncertain at work, but we would work it out. I'll help and I'm sure between us we'll manage."

I don't miss the tense tone in his voice as he says quickly, "No. I need to sort things at work first. Once this is all done and dusted, we can go from there. Until then, we carry on as normal."

I say nothing and he says softly. "I do love you though, Tia."

My heart flutters as I whisper, "I love you, too."

Just before he hangs up, I say quickly, "When do I get to see you again?"

"Come and meet me for lunch tomorrow. There's a hotel around the corner from the office that we can use for some privacy."

I'm excited at the mere thought of it and say happily, "I'll make sure to wear something you'll like."

He laughs and cuts the call and leaves me with a big grin on my face. Yes, Anthony likes me to dress up for him, and I have just the outfit in mind.

CHAPTER 2

VENETIA

"*V*enetia, I'm home."

My heart sinks as Matthew charges into the room and sweeps me off my feet. "I missed you. How was your trip?"

"Oh, you know, the usual boring routine."

I smile to myself as I picture just what I've been doing for the last couple of days. It's true, I was meant to work, but I managed to swap with another stewardess and spent the days I should have been at work ensconced in a hotel room with Anthony. He told Arabella he was on a business trip and we had two glorious days of uninterrupted pleasure where we could pretend we were a normal couple.

Matthew grins. "Well, I'm glad you're home, because I've got a surprise for you."

The alarm bells start ringing as he says happily, "I've sorted us a flight to Italy for a few days and booked an exclusive hotel. I figured we needed some time together, and what could be a more perfect way to spend our anniversary than in Rome?"

My heart sinks as I try to appear pleased. "Thanks, but what about work?"

He smiles triumphantly. "I called rostering and told them to accommodate it. I didn't give them a reason, and they didn't question it. Sometimes it's good being the boss."

He winks and I smile, but inside my stomach is churning. I don't want to go to Rome with him. If Anthony asked, I'd leap at the chance, but I no longer find Matthew attractive and I hate myself for it.

He heads towards the cupboard and pulls out two glasses and some champagne from the fridge. "Tonight, we celebrate your return because I'm fast realising we need to spend more time together. Rome is just the beginning because I intend to treat you at every opportunity and it begins with this house."

I stare at him in surprise. "This house."

He nods and looks around him critically. "I know you've been itching to get started on it, and I've always told you we couldn't afford it. Well, the end-of-year bonus has come in and there's more than enough to pay a designer to bring your dream to life."

He hands me the glass and says sweetly, "So, here's to our exciting future and the house of your dreams. You now have my full support to furnish it however you want and get the decorators in. Happy Anniversary, darling."

I can't help it and the tears fall and he looks at me with concern. "What's the matter? I thought you'd be happy."

Sniffing, I walk across and wrap my arms around him and say with actual emotion, "I don't deserve you."

He pulls back and lifts my face to his and kisses me so sweetly it reminds me of feelings I used to have. "I love you, Venetia, and I would do anything for you. I realise things have been a little tense between us for a while now, and I blame myself for that. I've held you back from doing what you wanted because of money. I've seen the way you look at your friend's houses and amazing things. I watch as they flash their wealth and you go without. Well, not anymore. I can tell how much it all means to you and now we have the money to make your dreams come true. So, drink up honey and then get dressed up because I'm taking you to Sergio's for dinner and spoiling you like I should have done ages ago."

He kisses me so sweetly and tenderly I feel a stirring of something that hasn't been there for some time. A flame that has almost burned out but has had new life fanning it into life again. As I kiss my husband, I taste something that's been missing for a long time now, but it's a familiar one that brings back sweet memories. This Matthew standing holding me so tenderly in his arms is the man I fell in love with and that has made an extremely complicated situation even more so because suddenly, I have my husband back and it's made me realise why I loved him in the first place.

* * *

Dinner was magical, interesting, and surprising. It was as if I was on a first date and the man opposite me was trying extra hard to impress. Matthew was funny, attentive and rather sexy and I found myself laughing along with him as we used to all those years ago. In fact, I completely forgot about Anthony, which was a feat in itself because he has been on my mind 24/7 ever since we started our affair.

As we walk from the restaurant, I am slightly guilty that I drank so much wine. I am pregnant after all and everybody knows you shouldn't drink while pregnant. But I am trying to forget about that because tonight I am me again. Venetia Stanmore, that young, vivacious woman, who had it all.

As Matthew takes my hand and helps me into the car, I smile up at him and realise that actually, I do have it all and I've been so shallow and selfish I never saw what was staring at me over the table every day. I already have the man I love and should never have started looking for him elsewhere.

We head back to The Chase and I am excited. Matthew was throwing me so many lustful looks, I am quite breathless about the night ahead. Perhaps we can rekindle the passion of our early months, and I experience a shiver of desire as I think about what that involves. We had an amazing sex life in the beginning and I am keen to revisit the memory. However, the sight that greets us is an unusual one as we see the blue lights flashing outside Miranda and James's house and Matthew says with alarm, "This doesn't look good. I hope nothing's happened."

I feel anxious as I stare at the lights and say fearfully, "Do you think they're ok? It can't be Miranda; she's gone to New York to see a... friend."

As I say the word, it leaves a nasty taste in my mouth. Despite the fact I've been doing the same thing for some time now, it's different when it's your friend and you know their husband. I'm a hypocrite because I am betraying my own friend and husband, but I appear blinded by love and can't see things clearly when it comes to my own situation.

Matthew says firmly, "Let's go and see if they're ok."

He pulls up and I say in a worried voice, "Do you think we should? They may not welcome our intrusion."

Matthew is already knocking on the door before the last word leaves my lips and, sighing, I make my way to join him.

James opens the door and I'm shocked at the sight of him. He looks red-eyed and dishevelled and so tired I fear the worst.

Matthew says in a kind voice, "Is everything ok mate?"

He shakes his head. "Not really. I came home and found I'd had an unwelcome visitor. The place has been ransacked, and all our valuables were stolen."

I gasp and glance across to our house. "Do you think we've all been hit?"

Matthew looks alarmed and James shrugs. "It may be wise

to check while the police are here. They think it happened earlier, so if you've been home already, probably not."

Matthew looks at me and smiles reassuringly. "I'm sure we're fine, but it would be wise to check. James, if you want to stay at our house tonight, you're more than welcome."

James shakes his head and says to my relief, "It's fine. As soon as the police get what they need, I'll probably just grab some supper and hit the hay."

We nod and leave him to it, and I grasp Matthew's hand fearfully. "He looked terrible."

Matthew shakes his head sadly. "I don't know what's going on there, but he's had that haunted expression in his eyes for months now."

I fall silent because I already know the reason. It's no secret his marriage to Miranda is crumbling. I suppose I never considered his feelings at all and I'm ashamed of myself for glossing over a situation that is actually devastating for the other person. Suddenly, I feel like the worst woman who ever lived because I am that person. Suddenly, I stop and say with a slight tremor in my voice, "I'm scared, Matthew."

He spins around and pulls me close, whispering, "It's ok, I'm here. I won't let anybody hurt you."

As I cling to my husband opposite my lover's house, the enormity of my situation hits me like a wrecking ball. What have I done?

CHAPTER 3

VENETIA

*T*he next morning, I wake up after a future changing night with my husband. When we returned from the restaurant, we rekindled our relationship in the bedroom and I could have wept when the old feelings came back with a vengeance and I realised what I had nearly destroyed by infatuation.

As Matthew headed off for work, I made up my mind. My fling with Anthony must end. It's not fair on any of us and should never have started in the first place so, I make the call I should have done at the beginning.

"Hey, Tia, looking forward to our lunch date with you being the lunch."

For some reason, my skin crawls and it surprises me. I thought he was everything I ever wanted and after only one night, he's now everything I don't want.

I lay awake last night after Matthew fell asleep and thought of Anthony. The way he pursued me at the beginning, with a few chosen words and flirtatious looks. He flattered me and made me feel special, where Matthew just took me for granted.

We met by chance one day in town and he offered to buy me lunch. I suppose I was always a little in awe of Anthony and Arabella. She appeared to be the model wife and their life seemed the stuff of fairy tales. My own marriage was becoming stale, and I wanted what they had. It didn't take much to reel me in and soon our flirting became a full-blown affair.

Heading back to reality, I say quickly, "I'm sorry, Anthony, there's been a change of plan."

"Why?"

"Matthew's getting suspicious and we should cool it for a while. I'll call you when the dust settles."

He sighs heavily. "Bother. I was looking forward to playing with my favourite girl. Are you sure you can't get away, even for a few hours? I'll make it worth your while?"

"No, I'm sorry. As I said, I'll call."

I pause and before saying quickly, "I'm sorry, I've got to go. Someone's at the door."

I hang up before he can say anything and exhale sharply. That was tense and I'm no fool. Anthony will immediately know something's up, but I can't help that.

* * *

Later in the afternoon, I notice Arabella returning from work and make a decision. I need to start building bridges, so I grab my keys and head across the road to see her.

A car is on the driveway and I experience a pang when I see the familiar sports car. Matthew felt sorry when her car was repossessed and offered to add her to the insurance of his spare two-seater. He uses it as a little run-around for the summer and he managed to convince her she would be doing him a favour in driving it. Once again, it makes me realise just how special he is. Always thinking of others where I apparently only think of myself. Well, not anymore because today is the start of the new me. It's time to take charge of my own destiny and I know where I want that to lie.

Arabella looks surprised when she answers the door and I say nervously, "I'm sorry, Arabella, I wondered if you had a minute."

She beckons me in and I follow her through the marble-tiled hallway to the fabulous state-of-the-art kitchen that is the envy of women everywhere.

"It's great to see you, Venetia. It's ages ago that we had a proper catch-up. Why don't I crack open a bottle of wine and we can put the world to rights?"

I perch on the barstool and say quickly, "I hope you don't mind me dropping by. I wanted to grab the number of the interior designer you use."

She looks surprised. "Of course, I have it in my address book. What are you planning?"

I say with excitement. "Matthew wants me to go ahead and design the house. He's received a huge bonus and has given me Carte blanche to get creative, along with a big, fat budget."

Arabella turns to me, her eyes shining. "Wow, you're so lucky. I love a good project and what better one than a whole house? If you need any help, I'll be glad to offer my services."

I feel bad as I witness the genuine warmth she gives me and feel like the worst person alive as I picture myself in bed with her husband, while she waits at home dealing with the fallout from his mistakes.

I grab the glass of wine and say brightly, "Thanks, I'll take you up on that."

She pours herself a glass and kicks off her shoes, sighing wearily. "I'm glad to get those off. You know, standing behind a desk all day is not for the faint-hearted."

I look at her with interest. "How is the job? It must be strange working after all these years."

"It is but I'm enjoying it way more than I should. The people are lovely and I'm having such a good time that I sometimes forget I'm being paid. I also get free membership, enabling me to continue with my classes and I also get subsidised meals and drinks."

She laughs. "How the worm has turned. Subsidised meals. Who'd have believed that a few months ago?"

I look at her with sympathy, and she smiles. "Don't feel bad. This is probably the best thing that's ever happened to me. I'm learning to be independent and now I have more in my life than just caring for Anthony."

At the mention of my lover, I almost spit out my wine and she says sadly, "I still can't believe what happened. You know, he's changed so much since he told me."

My heart thumps as I say a little too brightly, "How come?"

"Well, he no longer shows any interest in me. We are leading separate lives and I'm worried he's depressed and bottling it all up. Then what happened to Anton appeared to shake him up badly. I don't even know who he is anymore and have no way of helping him through this health scare because he won't talk to me about it. If I mention it, he gets angry and defensive and storms off to his study, telling me to mind my own business. To be honest, I'm at my wit's end and I am seriously considering seeking professional help."

Before I can even ask what she means by that, the doorbell rings and she looks at me with surprise. "I wonder who that could be? Wait here, I'll get rid of them."

I take another swig of my wine as I struggle to get my thumping heart under control. This is a disaster. If she ever found about my affair with Anthony, I would lose her friendship, which I'm fast realising means more to me than I thought it did.

I hear loud voices and move towards the door, and what I see makes my blood run cold.

Two policemen are standing in the hallway and I hear one of them say sternly, "I'm sorry, but you'll have to accompany us to the station."

I stare in shock as she turns and says in a frightened voice, "Venetia, call Anthony. The police are arresting me for burglary. Please call him."

I move towards them and the policeman says sternly, "Sorry, Miss. It's probably best you do as your friend asks."

I watch helplessly as Arabella leaves with them and my head spins. Burglary, what the…?

Quickly, I reach for my phone and dial Anthony's number and he answers in a curt voice, "So, you changed your mind then?"

"No, I mean, you have to come home quickly. It's Arabella."

I hear the panic in his voice, as he says quickly, "What about her?"

I whisper the words as if I can't quite believe I'm saying them. "She's been arrested."

"Arrested! For what?"

"Burglary."

"What the… I'm on my way."

He cuts the call and I find myself shivering as I try to get my head around what just happened. Arabella, a burglar, surely not.

CHAPTER 4

VENETIA

*I*n a daze, I wander around her impeccable home and note the tasteful furnishings and the way everything is in its place and how much it gleams. I've always loved Arabella's home and now I can look around uninterrupted while I wait for Anthony.

I move from room to room, really taking everything in and salivating over a home I would die to own myself.

I move into Anthony's study and inhale the intoxicating aroma of leather, wood panelling, and expensive aftershave. I sit in his leather chair and stare at the photographs on his polished desk looking out from their silver frames, of Arabella staring at him seductively. There is one of them on their wedding day and my mouth waters at how attractive Anthony looks. He is probably the sexiest man I have ever met, and the look he is giving her makes my heart flutter. Those eyes promise her a night to remember, and I know only too well what that means. I picture him kissing me all over and doing things to me that I never thought possible. I imagine his unshaven face in the morning as he leans over and kisses me like the demanding lover he is. I picture myself running my hands over his taut, hairy chest, as he nibbles my ear and I feel myself pant as I remind myself of just how good a lover he is.

Moving away, I head upstairs, taking in every smell and detail of this impressive home. I tread on the softest cream carpet as I climb the huge staircase that divides at the top, leading to a galleried landing.

As if on autopilot, I head towards their room and gasp at the romantic four-poster bed draped in ivory silk, with satin sheets and a crystal-encrusted coverlet. The pillows encourage you to lay your head on them and I picture how soft the fabric of the sheets would feel on my naked body as I wait for Anthony to give me the utmost pleasure.

Moving into her dressing room, I delight in the neatly arranged wardrobes filled with every type of garment imaginable. Glittering dresses sit alongside cashmere jumpers and fur coats. Rows upon rows of designer shoes are every woman wet dream and the handbags alone could keep a family in food for a year.

The floor to ceiling ornate mirrors reminds me what an imposter looks like as I stare at myself, looking green with envy. I want this. I want this life, but I no longer want her husband. Anthony does not measure up to Matthew because he is the kindest, most loving man that a woman could ever wish for. He may not be as devastatingly handsome as Anthony and he may not turn me on as much, but the more I learn about each man, the more I lean towards Matthew because he would never treat me the way Anthony is treating Arabella.

As I move into her bathroom, my eyes water at the number of expensive lotions and designer fragrances inside her mirrored cupboards. The fluffy white towels appear brand new and the air smells of expensive scented products that probably cost more than my month's wages. Then, as I open a drawer to peer inside, I see it. A pregnancy test. Not just one either. Several, in fact. Typical Arabella, who never does anything by half. She has bought out the shop, it seems, which speaks of a desperation I can't understand. She wants this. She wants a baby so badly she must run to test herself every time she has sex.

With the stick in my hand, I don't even think about it and do what I should have done weeks ago.

I take the test.

Five minutes seem like four hours and as I wait for the results, I wonder what I will do when it's confirmed. To be honest, I don't need clarification because I just know. I'm pregnant with Anthony's baby, and it's ironic that I'm finding out for sure in his wife's bathroom.

As the telltale blue line confirms my worst fears, I hear Anthony's car pull up in the driveway. As I stare at the line and my world explodes all around me, I note the sound of footsteps heading towards me.

"Venetia, where are you?"

I appear to be struck dumb because all I can do is try to organise the chaotic thoughts in my brain as they crowd to tell me what an idiot I am and as Anthony races into the bathroom and sees me holding the test, I stare at him in shock as he grabs it from my hand and says, "What the fuck? Is this what I think it is?"

I nod and stare at him, my eyes wide, and watch him detonate before my eyes.

"What the fuck? The stupid bitch, she knows I don't want kids, and she's gone behind my back and got herself pregnant without me knowing."

He starts pacing angrily and yells, "I can't believe it, I told her no. No! You hear me? She couldn't even give me that. The things I have done for that woman. You can see how much I've given her. Look around you, Venetia. Is this the home of a woman who goes without? Pregnant, for Christ's sake; I could murder her with my bare hands. I'm not ready to be a father and she had better agree to an abortion because I'm putting my foot down."

I stare at him in shock, as he rants while pacing around the overly large bathroom. Then he stops and turns and the gleam in his eyes makes my blood run cold as he says, "She's been arrested?"

I nod, too afraid to speak, and he laughs softly. "Then that's the best place for her. Let the bitch stew in a cell for a few hours and think about what she's done. Did you say burglary?"

I nod again and he looks thoughtful. "Interesting. In fact, very interesting. I wonder what my devious wife has been up to behind my back? Maybe this is her new job and not the one at the country club."

Suddenly, his eyes soften and he beckons me over. "Come here."

I swallow hard and say in a brittle voice, "Why?"

His eyes narrow and I recognise the look. Anthony is so turned on right now, which makes me breathless. I can't help it and just the sight of him makes my legs weak and my body shakes with need.

He growls, "Come over here and I'll show you what you've been missing. How about it, honey? Have you ever fantasised about us in my marital bed? Have you ever wished you were in her place and imagined us as a couple waking up beside each other every day?"

I whimper as he crosses the room and removes his jacket, holding my eyes with his, as he stares at me with a need that takes my breath away. Right now, I have forgotten every-thing. I can't even remember my own name as I'm caught up in his spell. Anthony has me so hooked there's no use in struggling because at this moment, in this room and in this state of mind, I ditch my principles in a heartbeat and go to him like the whore I am. Yes, Anthony knows exactly how to appeal to the weakest part of me because as I remove my clothes and stand naked before him, I know I'm fucked before he even touches me.

CHAPTER 5

VENETIA

*I*t's all around the Chase in a matter of hours. Arabella has been arrested for burgling Miranda and James's home. I think we're in shock and as Matthew and I head towards James's house to check if he's ok, Miranda returns home.

She pulls up in the driveway and looks at us in surprise.

"Hey guys, it's good to see you."

I stare at her and note the brightness in her eyes and the red tinge to her cheeks. She looks utterly amazing and I can tell immediately—she's in love.

She kisses us both on the cheek and Matthew gallantly offers to fetch her suitcases in and as she unlocks the door, she whispers, "I'll fill you in later. Best trip I've ever had."

She giggles and I say awkwardly, "Um, Miranda, I think there's something you should know."

However, the door opens before I can fill her in and James stands there looking at her with what appears to be mixed emotions. I note how awkward they appear to be with one another and share a look with Matthew as Miranda says softly, "Hello, James."

166

He nods and smiles. "You're back then."

She laughs a little self-consciously. "Is that the best you can do?"

He appears to shake himself and moves toward her and kisses her on both cheeks before realising we're standing there.

"Oh, hi guys, did you want something?"

Matthew says a little awkwardly, "Just checking if you are ok. We heard about..."

He stops and looks a little uncomfortable and Miranda says in surprise, "What's going on?"

Sighing, James runs his fingers through his hair and says gruffly, "You had better come inside."

Matthew says quickly, "We'll leave you to it. Just knock if you need us."

Miranda follows James, looking worried, and Matthew pulls me away, whispering, "Not much of a homecoming, is it?"

"Not really, but I'm sure Miranda can cope."

I think of my friend and am a little annoyed, although I have no right to. After what happened earlier today with Anthony, I've been so angry with myself. I've sunk to a new all-time low because I loved every minute of what we did in Arabella's bed. While she was at the police station, probably worried sick, I was living out my fantasy with her husband, who I have now decided that I hate with a passion. After seeing his reaction to what he thought was Arabella's pregnancy, it changed everything. He isn't ready to be a father, just as I'm not ready to be a mother, so as hard as it will be, I've made up my mind and first thing tomorrow, I'm making an appointment to visit Doctor Shrovesbury. I'm getting my mistake dealt with and wiping all traces of Anthony Adams from my life.

As I take Matthew's hand, the tears build behind my eyes

because I almost jeopardised everything. Matthew Stanmore is worth a thousand Anthony's and I nearly made the biggest mistake of my life.

The next day, as soon as Matthew leaves for work, I start sorting myself out. As soon as the doctor's opened, I rang for an appointment later on today and set about cleaning my home. First things first, I will deal with the pregnancy and then I need to start planning my new interior.

I'm interrupted by a knock on the door and am not surprised to see Miranda standing there looking extremely worried.

Beckoning her inside, she follows me, saying shakily, "It's terrible, Arabella's been arrested for burgling our house; I can't believe it."

I flick the kettle on and nod. "I know. I don't believe it either. Do you think it's true?"

She shakes her head and says emphatically, "No, it's preposterous."

I nod. "I thought so too, but what if she snapped? I mean, she's going through a very tough time and it happens. They have no money and perhaps she saw this as a way of making some."

Miranda says angrily, "Why would she do that to me? No, they've got the wrong person."

I stare at her in surprise because she seems so adamant and I have a little more respect for the woman standing before me. She has an unwavering trust that I don't share. When I found out, I thought it must be true. In fact, I was quite pleased in a sick way because it knocked a little of the shine off the woman who, in my eyes, could do no wrong. I was strangely excited to learn what was going to happen and now I feel like the worst bitch in the world.

Miranda looks so worried I smile reassuringly. "I'm sure

you're right, and it's a mistake. Anthony will make sure she gets the best lawyer and she'll be home before you know it."

"She is home."

"Since when?"

Sighing, Miranda nervously taps her fingers on the counter. "The police called and told James she'd been released. Apparently, they found some of our items in a nearby pawnshop, and the manager told them they had been left by a woman calling herself Arabella Adams. That's why they put two and two together and arrested her. However, late last night, the man was called in to verify that she was the woman in his shop by way of an identity parade. He said the woman wasn't there, although Arabella did seem quite familiar, so they let her go for now."

I exhale sharply. "Wow, that's some story. Maybe it was her, and she had a wig on? That may have thrown the man."

Shrugging, Miranda reaches for the coffee and I say sympathetically, "It must have been a shock though, coming home to all this. Did you lose anything dear to you?"

"Not really. They were mainly James's things, luckily. His mother's jewellery, watches, you know, the sort of thing."

Suddenly, she looks a little brighter and says with excitement, "I haven't told you about my trip."

I have a bitter taste in my mouth as she says dreamily, "Miles and I are in love. You know, Venetia, I was a little worried about going to another country to visit a man I had met for a few minutes, but it was like an amazing dream. He made sure I travelled first class and had a limo waiting for me at the airport. It whisked me away to an amazing apartment overlooking Central Park, and he was there waiting. Oh my God, he was sexier than I remembered and showed me what I've been missing out on all these years. During the day he worked because he runs a large company, but at night, well, let's just say New York is very hot this time of year."

She giggles, "To be honest, I'm surprised I can still walk. We didn't hold back and I'm a little grateful to come home for the rest."

I take in her heightened colour and bright eyes. She looks so excited and I understand that feeling. Maybe it's the fact it's forbidden and the intrigue and sheer danger involved that gets the pulse racing so much, but I know only too well, it's a drug that is difficult to live without.

She stares dreamily into space and says in a soft voice, "I've only come home to tie things up with James because Miles has asked me to move in with him and I'd be a fool not to."

I had sort of guessed this was going to be the outcome and say sadly, "Poor James."

She looks at me with a frown. "What's poor about James? He's only got himself to blame. If he wasn't such a bore, I wouldn't have felt the need to go looking for my excitement elsewhere. No, I'm moving on, which means he can too. He'll be ok, the insurance will pay up for the items stolen, and he's got a good job and will just carry on as before. We weren't much of a couple anyway and now he's free to meet someone like him and will probably be happy in the long run. Between me and you, James and I stopped having sex months ago, so I'm doing him a favour, really."

She shrugs and looks at her watch. "Anyway, I have things to do and the first one is to go and check that Fleur's ok."

"Fleur? I didn't know she was home."

Miranda smiles. "I saw her car in the driveway when I woke up this morning. It appears that we're all back together again, so maybe we should meet up later and have a catch-up. I would say come to mine, but James will be there and I won't be able to talk freely. Perhaps Fleur will do the honours?"

She jumps up and heads for the door before turning and

saying sweetly, "You know, Venetia, I must say you're looking amazing, glowing in fact. What happened to you since I've been gone because you certainly didn't look so good the night we went out?"

I smile and feel warm inside as I say, "Matthew and I are back on. I've realised that what I've been looking for was here all along. He's realised it too and now all we want is to make our life together and that suits me just fine."

Miranda stares at me keenly and smiles. "I'm glad one of us is happy. Well, make that two when I sort things out with James. You know, fate works in mysterious ways and who would have believed all this would happen in such a short space of time? As hard as it is at the moment, it will all work out good in the end. I just know it."

She smiles and leaves and I think about what she told me. Will it all work out for the best? I certainly hope so because after the last few weeks, I'm not sure if I can cope with any more dramas.

CHAPTER 6

VENETIA

*B*efore I head to the doctors, I pay Fleur a visit and am shocked when she answers the door. She looks so tired and strained, and yet she smiles when she sees me and hugs me warmly. "Venetia. You look amazing. Come on in."

I follow her into her perfect house and gaze around me with envy. Like Arabella's home, Fleurs has everything I've ever wanted. I always considered it a little vulgar because it's stuffed with more material wealth than any person has the right to own, but now all I see is a palace.

She offers me a coffee but I say quickly, "No thanks, I have an appointment in town to get to but wanted to check on you first."

She smiles sadly. "I'm getting there. It was good to get away, but I knew I'd have to return at some point. It's hard though."

Nodding, I glance around. "It must be. I don't know if I could cope if it happened to me."

Fleur's bottom lip quivers and it breaks my heart. The usually in control, slightly ferocious young woman, seems so vulnerable and as if all her hard edges have been worn away. She is still incredibly beautiful, even in grief and I smile softly, "Where did you go?"

I'm not sure if it's my imagination or not, but she appears a little uncomfortable, before saying quickly, "Just to stay with a friend. Anyway, I wanted to ask you over tonight. All of you, Matthew included. I thought I'd throw a little coming home party and want to fill the house with laughter once again."

I stare at her in surprise. "A party?"

She nods, but I notice won't look me in the eye. "Yes, I thought we all needed cheering up and to clear the air."

Smiling, I nod. "Great, what time?"

"Make it eight o'clock. That gives the workers a chance to have supper and then we can all feel relaxed. I don't know about you, but it seems like ages ago that we all did. In fact, I can't remember the last time. Anyway, we'll catch up later. Thanks for dropping by."

As I turn to leave, she says sadly, "Terrible business about Arabella. What do you make of it?"

"I don't know. I mean, I don't want to believe it and it sounds like a case of mistaken identity, anyway. It was probably a professional who has been watching the house for weeks."

Fleur nods before saying sharply, "I'm not so sure."

"What do you mean?" I say in surprise.

"Well, think about it. There are four homes here, all equal in every way. Apparently, nobody was in that day so why would the thief only target one house? Surely, if, as you say, they had been watching the place, they would have seen everyone leave. It was a golden opportunity to clean up and yet they only targeted one house and only took jewellery. I think there's more to this story than meets the eye, which is why the police let Arabella go."

Nodding, I say with interest. "Have you seen her - Arabella?"

Fleur nods sadly. "As soon as I got here. She came over late last night and we spent most of the night talking it through. You know, she's had such a terrible time and I'm really worried about her."

I feel utterly terrible, as I say guiltily, "Yes, me too."

I'm not sure if it's just my guilty conscience, but I'm convinced Fleur knows because she says tightly, "Yes, well, I'm sure it will all come out in the end. Arabella will be fine; I'll make sure of it."

Feeling a little uncomfortable, I head to the door and Fleur smiles. "Thanks for coming, Venetia. Have a good day and I'll see you later."

As I walk to my car, I'm on edge. I'm not sure why but something tells me I'm not going to enjoy Fleur's get together later on this evening and I only hope I'm proved wrong because now I've made my decision, I don't want anything to get in the way of my happy ever after with Matthew.

* * *

The doctor couldn't have been more helpful and yet, as I walk back to my car after having arranged a suitable date for the termination, I feel strange. I suppose I went into this treating it like a problem that needed dealing with, but now it's sorted, I am uneasy about my decision. I never regarded my pregnancy as involving an actual life before and something happened when I sat in the chair opposite the doctor. I was strangely protective.

Now, as I sit in my car, I run my hand across my stomach and picture the little life forming inside. The tears sting behind my eyes and I fight the urge to cry. What's happening to me? I don't want this baby, of course I don't, but somehow, I keep on picturing the little bundle of innocence that my sins created. A baby boy, or girl, equal parts Anthony and me and then it hits me. What if it's Matthew's?

Stunned, I sit back with my head against the rest and my world shakes again. It could be. It could be my husband's because even though we hadn't had sex as much lately, we still did. What if this baby is our baby and I just signed its death warrant?

My mind races as I start the car to drive into town. What if it is? Do I want it? Does this change everything? Yes, it does, because if this baby is mine and Matthew's, I want it more than anything.

My phone rings as I pull into a parking space in town and with a sinking feeling, I see it's Anthony. I answer with impatience, "Yes?"

He laughs softly. "Is that it, darling? What happened to the sultry greeting I'm used to?"

I say somewhat irritably, "What do you want, Anthony?"

His voice is laced with steel as he says, "I need to see you. Meet me at the Costa by the bridge in twenty minutes."

"How do you know I can make it?"

He laughs, "Because I know everything, Venetia. I'm aware you're in town and not far from the bridge."

I peer around me fearfully and whisper, "How do you know?"

I can almost see the wicked glint in his eye as he says triumphantly, "Because I saw you park up. I'm having my hair cut opposite and recognised your car. I should be done in ten minutes, so you can go and get the coffees in."

I sigh irritably. "Ok, twenty minutes but Anthony..."

"Yes, Venetia."

"It will be the last time."

I'm surprised when he laughs and says firmly, "I know and that's what I wanted to say. Things have changed and we need to draw a line under this... um... friendship."

He cuts the call and I stare at my phone in shock. Friendship! Is this what this was to him - a friendship?

As I purchase my parking ticket, I sense my rage building. A friendship! That's all this was to him. I loved him, really loved him. I wanted a future with this man and in one sentence he resorted our affair to just a fling, a bit on the side that was never going anywhere. I'm not sure why I feel so affronted. Surely this is the best possible outcome of an extremely bad situation, but it doesn't make me feel good about myself. That's all I was, a distraction, a bit of fun, and now he's decided he's had enough.

As I reach the coffee shop, I join the line and think about what's happened. We have been foolish, cruel and irresponsible and, above all, disloyal. I actually couldn't hate myself more than I do at this moment because I now regret every minute I ever spent obsessing about the utter creep and disgusting human being that's about to finish with me. It hurts because I wanted to be the one to finish this, not him just so I could claw a little of my self-respect back.

As soon as I see him enter the shop, I hate the fact my pulse rate increases and the desire floods through me because there is no denying the fact that Anthony Adams is one sexy man. He sees me watching him and smirks as he saunters over and sits down beside me, leaning in and kissing me on the cheek. "Hey, you look amazing, darling."

I squirm on my seat because this feels so wrong, yet the pressure of his leg against mine reminds me that my body is still insanely attracted to him, even though my mind can't stand him.

He picks up the coffee I bought for him and says gratefully, "Thanks. I need this."

I say dully, "So, why did you want to meet?"

He smiles gently. "We need to cool this, and I expect you feel the same."

I nod as he sighs heavily. "It's been fun, but I need to step up and be the husband Arabella deserves. She's been through hell these last few months, and now I need to make things right."

I say tartly, "Why the concern now? Surely, she needed you before; what's changed?"

His eyes narrow and he looks at me with a hard expression. "Because what we did yesterday doesn't sit well with me. We had sex in the bed I share with my wife, who, despite everything, I love with my whole heart. When I went to the police station and saw her there, it hit me. She doesn't deserve any of this, and I need to make it right."

I roll my eyes and say sharply, "Such a loving husband, Anthony. I'm sure she doesn't deserve you."

His eyes flash. "Cut the smart remark. We both knew this was never going anywhere."

I am so hurt inside but won't give him the satisfaction of seeing it, so I say with an acid tongue, "So, why the sudden concern? Have you had your cake and made yourself sick on it because you seemed pretty keen yesterday?"

He smiles and I melt under the heat in his gaze. "I loved you in my own way, Tia. You were exactly what I needed at a difficult time. Our affair was amazing and made me feel more alive than ever, but we both knew that's all it was ever going to be. I mean, who wouldn't want a wife like Arabella? She's beautiful, kind and loyal. Our sex life is amazing, and she cares for me even though I don't deserve it. On the other hand, you're exciting, enticing and a bit of danger. The match that lights my flame and together we're so hot we nearly got burned. No, this is best all-round because if we allow us to destroy what we have with our spouses, we would destroy our own lives because as lovers we're electric but as partners, we would clash terribly. We are too fiery and too alike to work well together. You need Matthew just as much as I need Arabella. A steady rock to ground us and give our selfish lives meaning. It was amazing while it lasted, but it needs to end now."

As I nod and take a sip of my drink, I feel strange. This is the best outcome of a terrible mistake, yet what I had with Anthony was the stuff of dreams. Sitting so close to him makes me a little sad that this is the last time and I say sadly, "It was fun, though."

He nods and squeezes my hand. "Yes, it was. I'll never forget it, but we can't make the same mistake again. This will always be our secret—an amazing one, but we need to both grow up and take responsibility for the people we love and make things right."

He smiles sadly and makes to leave and I pull him down and say emotionally, "I do love Arabella too and am so sad about what we've done."

He smiles ruefully. "I feel the same about Matthew. It's one thing fooling around with each other, but another thing betraying our friends as well as the people we love. I don't know about you, Tia, but it's going to take me a long time to come to terms with what we did."

As he stands, I say hesitatingly, "What about the baby?"

He shrugs. "I'm not sure. I know Arabella is desperate to have one, but I'm not ready. I'm going to talk it through with her if the subject comes up, but until then, I'm going to bury my head in the sand and hope it all goes away."

As he turns to leave, I say nothing. That just about sums him up, spineless and self-absorbed. Arabella doesn't deserve a man like him and Matthew doesn't deserve a woman like me, and I vow to spend the rest of my life making it up to him.

"You are stunning. I almost wish we weren't going tonight."

I smile as I spray my favourite scent and smile at my husband. "You're not looking so bad yourself."

He grins and my heart flutters. Yes, Matthew Stanmore is the husband of my dreams. Good looking, kind, funny and caring. Who wouldn't want a man like that and I am incredibly lucky to have him? I certainly dodged a bullet with Anthony and as the fortune teller's words come back for another unwelcome visit, I turn my back on them for good. I have no future she said, well, now I have the brightest future because I have a husband I adore and a baby on the way. Yes, I'm keeping our baby because I know in my heart it's ours, mine and Matthew's and I'm not going to let any doubts creep in because even if it isn't, it won't matter. Matthew will never know and will raise this child anyway and love it as much as I do because he's just that kind of guy. I am the luckiest woman in the world and I nearly destroyed everything by seeing something I thought I wanted and placed it above the dream I already had.

Matthew walks over and wraps his arms around my waist and kisses my neck lovingly. "I love you, Venetia, and I can't wait to show you over and over again what that means on our trip to Rome."

Spinning around, I kiss him tenderly and am excited when I think about our trip tomorrow. Yes, as anniversaries go, this one will be the best one ever because now my marriage vows kick in and I will spend the rest of my life making the man I love the happiest man alive.

PART V

THE TEN COMMANDMENTS

CHAPTER 1

ARABELLA

I am broken. Being arrested was the final straw, and I waited for what seemed a lifetime for Anthony to come and rescue me from hell.

The police were sure it was me and, despite answering all their questions with ease; they remained unconvinced. They thought they had all the evidence they needed. The man in the pawnshop gave them my name, and I was the last one to leave The Chase that day.

It was only after the identity parade that they reluctantly let me leave without charge. Anthony was waiting and I remember falling into his arms and sobbing as if my heart would break. His arms held me tightly, and he whispered that everything would be ok and I longed to believe him. But how can they be? We have lost everything and now it appears I could lose my freedom as well because if the police get their way, they will arrest me again for a crime I didn't commit.

When I wake the next day, I have many questions needing answers and as Anthony spreads marmalade on his toast, I say sharply, "What took you so long yesterday?"

He smiles ruefully. "I'm sorry, darling, I didn't get Venetia's message for a few hours because I was in a meeting and had told my secretary I didn't want to be disturbed."

I sigh. "I was so afraid. I didn't know where you were and the police were so… scary."

He smiles sadly. "I'll never forgive myself. I can't believe they thought it was you in the first place. What was it they said, some woman with your name pawned the items and did it regularly? Are you sure there's something you're not telling me, darling?"

He throws me a sharp look and I am irritated beyond belief. "Of course not. I didn't do it. Why would I? I love Miranda and James and would never even think about breaking into another person's home and stealing from them. You should know that more than anybody, Anthony."

He stands up and pulls me into his arms, saying softly, "I know you would never do that. I'm sorry, darling, I love you and things are going to change around here."

Pulling back, I stare at him in surprise. "What do you mean – change?"

He winks. "All in good time. When I get back from work this evening, I may have some news. Clear your schedule and we'll talk."

As he turns away, I say quickly, "Don't forget we have Fleur's get together. We may not have time to talk."

He sighs irritably. "Then I'll get home early and we'll talk then. There's something I need to say and it won't wait."

He heads off to get ready, leaving me feeling curious. I wonder what it is he's got to tell me. I hope its good news because I could use some right now because once again, my period made an unwelcome appearance. I feel the depression hit me that's never far away, as I contemplate yet another month that I'm not pregnant. It's too much. Anthony and I haven't had sex in ages, so it's no wonder, really. He has been so distant and cold lately and today was the first time I saw traces of the man I married. Then again, there's the burglary. I can't believe they thought it was me, but they seemed so sure. I wonder who this Arabella Adams is that's been pawning stuff because it sure as hell wasn't me?

I'm glad that Fleur's home because I needed her and only realised how much when she went away. It was good to talk to her when I got back from the station last night because Anthony was in a terrible mood and stormed off almost as soon as he dropped me home. This morning though, it's as if he's a different person—the old Anthony I married, and I wonder what happened between dropping me off last night and waking up beside him this morning.

However, I don't have long to dwell on it because I'm due at work in an hour and need to get ready.

As soon as I step foot inside the country club, I relax. Here there are no problems to deal with that affect me. The people are kind and sweet and mainly good-tempered. I never imagined how much I would enjoy working and am grateful that Darren put a good word in for me.

It must be around eleven when I see the man himself and he saunters over and smiles sweetly. "How are things, Arabella?"

"Good thanks. I haven't seen you in ages, Darren. I heard you were off for a while; did you go away?"

"No, I just took a week off to spend with family and friends."

He gets called away and I sigh inside. He is certainly impressive and I can't help but admire the sight of his fit body in the lycra he wears so well. Despite being drop-dead gorgeous, he's also a nice guy too. Most of the women here fancy him to bits and I wonder if he has a special someone to go home to at night.

I am interrupted by the phone and turn my attention back to the reason I'm here.

The day passes quickly and around three o'clock I'm happy to notice a familiar face, although it is a little awkward. "Hi, Miranda. You look amazing. Did you have a good trip?"

I'm not sure if it's me, but she looks at me sheepishly and smiles. "Yes, thank you, the best, although my homecoming was a little shocking."

I blush as she shakes her head and says somewhat angrily, "I told them it was preposterous. There is no way you would ever do such a thing, and I am beyond angry on your behalf."

I smile with relief. "I'm glad you feel that way because, of course, it wasn't me. I wonder who it was though, because by the sounds of it, someone was using my identity, either that, or I have a double walking around."

Miranda nods. "It appears so. Anyway, hopefully, that's an end to it and the police will move onto more important things. You know, it's not so bad. James has lost a few trinkets, but will get the money back. I don't know what all the fuss is about, really."

I'm surprised at her words because, in her shoes, I would be devastated that anyone had even set foot inside my home, let alone rifled through my prized possessions. I peer at her carefully. "Do you feel strange knowing someone's been in your home?"

She shrugs and looks unconcerned. "Not really. I wasn't there, and neither was James, so there was no real harm done. I have much more important things on my mind because I've met someone."

I stare at her in shock and she giggles. "Don't look so

shocked Arabella, it's no secret my marriage was over a long time ago. No, I've met a man I'm crazy about and just as soon as I've sorted things out here, I'm heading back to New York and paradise."

She laughs at the expression on my face and says smugly, "No, my future is looking bright because Miles Sullivan is everything I've ever wanted in a man. Good looking, rich and good in bed. He's attentive, spoils me unashamedly, and is successful in every way. To be honest, I can't get back there fast enough, which is why I need to cancel my membership here."

I stare at her in shock and as if on autopilot, bring her details up on the screen and follow the steps necessary to cancel her membership. It's a little strange doing so because Miranda has been part of my life for a few years now and if she's right about things, is about to leave us all for good.

Once the formalities are completed, I say sadly, "I'm going to miss you. Please stay in touch."

Her face softens. "You must come and stay. You'll love New York and you'll love Miles. He's a fantastic man and once you meet him, you'll understand why this is so easy for me."

She smiles and says brightly, "Anyway, we'll get a chance to catch up at Fleur's later. I can't wait, although I'm not sure if James will make it."

"Why?"

She seems a little worried. "Because I'm going to tell him I'm leaving him as soon as he gets home and between me and you, he's been struggling for a while now and may drown his sorrows in the bottle. It's not great timing, but I can't think about his needs when my own are so much more fun."

She winks as she heads off, leaving me in shock. James is drinking! What can be so terrible to send him down that road and why is Miranda being such a selfish bitch? Surely, he doesn't deserve this on top of whatever else he's struggling with. I view my friend through a different pair of eyes and I don't like what I see. Maybe it's a good thing she's leaving because, by the sounds of it, James could do with meeting someone else, anyway.

CHAPTER 2

ARABELLA

"*A*rabella, are you there?"

My heart flutters as I hear Anthony calling as he returns home from work. I know he has something to tell me and I steel myself for whatever it is because the last time he had news; it was devastating.

I call out, "I'm in the bedroom."

I hear him pounding up the stairs and my heart pounds as I wonder what he's about to say. I pull my satin robe around me as if it will arm me with a barrier of protection against his words, as I prepare for the party in just a couple of hours' time.

As he enters the room, the look he shoots me is one I haven't seen for some time. Lust. He crosses the room and takes me in his arms and pulls me tight, saying huskily, "I'm so sorry, my darling, can you ever forgive me?"

Then, without waiting for a reply, he crashes his lips to mine and kisses me so hard I'm sure he will bruise my lips.

He runs his hand underneath my robe and groans. "I've missed you so much."

Feeling a little worried, I pull back and say fearfully, "Forgive you for what?"

He sighs and pulls me next to him on the bed and clasps my hand in his. "I've got a confession to make."

My heart starts thumping madly and I say fearfully, "What?"

He sighs heavily. "I lied to you."

I say nothing and wait for him to speak because my mind is racing at a million miles an hour as I wonder what I'm about to hear.

"The job - I never lost it."

I stare at him in shock, and he smiles ruefully. "It was all an act, a pretence, research for a show that's just got the go-ahead."

I struggle to understand what he's saying, and he laughs softly. "I can tell this has come as quite a shock. I always knew it would be but a happy one, I hope. I had to keep you in the dark, as did the rest of the production team, because we weren't the only ones trialling this. They also went through the same charade with their families and we documented every reaction, every consequence and have made it into the most explosive programme we have ever done. You should be proud, darling, because 'Living the Dream' is about to become a reality and make us more money than we have ever had in our lives."

My heart pounds as Anthony looks at me with so much pride and joy on his face, I almost can't breathe. Every word he just said races around my head as I try to take them in and make sense of them.

Taking my silence as relief, he says brightly, "You will receive your Porsche back tomorrow and you can resign from that job of yours. I've also booked us an all-inclusive five-star holiday to The Maldives to celebrate."

Finally, I find my voice and say in a whisper, "What about

your illness? Was that a lie?"

The expression on his face confirms it, and he appears a little contrite. "I'm sorry - yes. I've never been fitter actually and quite honestly, this project has invigorated me and made me hungry for more. I can't tell you how many times I've longed to confide in you, but couldn't. That's why I kept my distance for fear of slipping up. It was also the reason I called your parents." He laughs. "I know you hate them with a passion and it was interesting studying the effect they had on you. I must say, I was proud of you for stepping up and putting them in their place."

He must see the expression on my face because he says gently, "Don't you see why it had to be this way? The research we gathered has reinforced the fact this show will be dynamite and once you've got over the shock, I'm sure you'll agree with me."

I can't even cry. I can't even shout and I can't even speak because I'm not sure what emotion to deal with first. Relief, anger, tears or recriminations. I feel so badly betrayed I am struggling to make sense of my emotions. Anthony just smiles happily and sets about changing for the party tonight and I can tell he's reverted right back to the man he was before this whole charade.

As if on autopilot, I start getting ready myself and try to process my thoughts because now is not the time to deal with this. I need time to digest what he told me and come to terms with the fact that this whole nightmare was all a pretence.

By the time we head downstairs to make our way across the road to Fleur's, it's as if the last few months never happened. Normal service has resumed, at least in Anthony's eyes, but I see things very differently. I wonder how this will really end because I know I'm not finished with him yet, by a long way.

CHAPTER 3

MIRANDA

*A*s soon as I finish sorting out my things, I gaze around me with a small tinge of regret. I was so happy when we moved here. I thought this was everything I ever wanted - that James was everything I ever wanted and I'm shocked at how quickly things changed. James withdrew from me over time and I had no meaning in my life. I had given up my job, although I hardly missed that. No, it was much more fun playing at being the 'stay at home wife' and that would have been enough if my husband was like Anthony or Matthew. Even Anton was a better husband to Fleur, and they weren't actually married. No, James has been withdrawn for some time now and I didn't care enough to find out why.

As I place the last of the things I want to take with me into the large, wheeled suitcase, I glance at them and laugh to myself. It's a good job that travelling first class gives you a bigger baggage allowance, although Miles did say he would pay the excess if I brought more than I was allowed.

As I think about Miles, I hug myself with excitement. How did I get so lucky? He is surely the dream. The one we all hope to meet and the one who won't let me down like James. Don't ask me how I know, but I do. Yes, Miles is my Prince Charming, and I am booked on a flight first thing tomorrow to deliver me to my happily ever after.

Humming to myself, I peer at myself critically in the mirror. Yes, this Chanel pantsuit looks as amazing as it did on the model in Saks. Miles isn't James and gave me free rein with his credit card. He told me to go mad, so I did and felt like Julia Roberts in Pretty Woman, as I had a great time filling the walk-in closet in his penthouse with many designer outfits.

Now all I need to do is tell James I'm leaving him.

I head downstairs to his dimly lit study and knock firmly on the door before heading inside. In the lamplight, I notice James bent over another sheaf of papers and feel a stirring of fondness for the dusty barrister. He looks up and I note the brightness of his eyes as mine fall to the half-empty glass beside him. I shake my head and say softly, "Still drinking, I see."

He nods and pushes the glass away. "Yes, it's the only way I can cope with a nightmare."

I sit opposite him and say gently, "We both know what I'm about to say. I'm sure it won't come as a shock to you."

He nods and I stare at the broken man before me as he says, "When?"

"Tomorrow. I'm packed and ready to go and I just wanted to say, I don't want anything from you."

He looks up in surprise, and I shrug. "To be honest, James, you've given me more than enough over the years. I haven't earned my share of this house, and I wouldn't want to cause you any more upheaval."

I am shocked to see the tears welling up in his eyes as he says in a whisper, "Thank you."

I'm not sure when James broke, but he is. Broken beyond

repair and suddenly I'm fearful of his mental state. I say gently, "You need to get help, James. Tell me, what happened with the court case?"

He smiles sadly. "A fine and banned for a year."

I'm relieved. "I'm glad. Perhaps now you can move on and deal with the drinking."

He shakes his head. "You're right. I am sorry though, Miranda, for everything."

I'm puzzled as I wonder what he means, and he shakes his head.

"I haven't been a good husband to you and I'm not surprised you're leaving me. May I ask where you're going?"

"New York."

He nods. "Ah, I thought as much. Is it another man?"

I laugh incredulously, "Of course, why wouldn't it be? I wouldn't leave you unless I had another man."

He laughs softly. "There she is, the Miranda I know and once loved."

"Once loved?"

He nods. "You changed, my dear. As soon as you got bored, you lost interest. I've known for ages we were drifting apart. You no longer wanted me and, as it turns out, I never wanted you either."

His words shock me as I suddenly face the fact that perhaps James had someone else all along. I'm not sure I like the feeling that hits me and I say sharply, "So, what are you saying?"

He smiles, but it has a sadness to it that brings tears to my eyes. "I fell in love, Miranda, but it didn't work out."

Now I understand what the expression was in his eyes that faced me every day and despite my anger at learning he had an affair; I have compassion for the fact he lost her. "What happened?"

He looks at me awkwardly and I wonder if it's someone I know.

Then he says a name I never expected to hear in a million years. "It was Anton."

It's as if all the air has been sucked out of the room as I struggle to understand what he just said. "Anton!"

He nods and I'm shocked as the tears falling freely down his face.

"We never meant for it to happen. I'm not even sure how it started, but one day we were talking and then something clicked between us and the next thing I knew we were kissing and well... I'm sure you don't want to hear the rest."

I squeeze my eyes tightly shut as I try to breathe. Anton! I can't believe it, James is gay - Anton was gay; this is devastating.

He carries on regardless and says with emotion. "We fell in love, but both struggled in our own way. I think he was disgusted with his feelings for me and what we felt compelled to do every time we met. We tried at every opportunity to end it, but kept coming back for more."

I want to put my hands over my ears and make him stop, but he carries on, as seemingly now he's started, he can't stop. "We fell in love and yet we both knew it would end in disaster. He used to meet me at the office after training, or in a nearby hotel room. We were careful but infatuated and couldn't get enough of each other. It was pure torture watching each other in company, knowing we only wanted to be together and I couldn't see a way out of the situation we were in. It affected us both in different ways and I started drinking to dull the pain. He got angry and started picking fights with the guys from work. Then it started."

"What started?"

I almost can't breathe as James's face contorts with rage and he spits, "Someone found out. We both received a video of us taken from a hotel we loved to meet at. I'm not sure who it was, possibly one of the staff who recognised Anton, but we both received the video of us having sex and a demand for money. We were told to pay up or risk public humiliation. The barrister and the footballer. It would make for damaging headlines, so we paid the money."

The blood rushes to my head as I picture what they went through. Then everything falls into place as I say sadly, "That's why you were so tight with money, wasn't it?"

He nods. "I tried to keep up with the demands but was falling behind. I couldn't tell you and so, I did the best I could. Anton paid the most because he could afford to, but then he discovered who it was and went to confront them."

I hold my breath as James breaks down before my eyes. "He wound up dead in his swimming pool and I never got to find out what happened. I lost the man I love in the most secret and tragic of ways. The only good thing that came out of it was the demands stopped overnight. Anton had done what he said he would do and made the problem go away. However, I never knew it would be at a cost I would never have paid – his life."

As he breaks down again, I rush to comfort him. We may no longer be together, but I do love James in my own way. His story has broken my heart and I can't believe I never noticed the pain he was going through. I put my own selfish desires above his well-being and I will never forgive myself.

As I rock James in my arms as he cries like a baby, so much sadness washes over me. I can't leave him like this. I must step up and do the right thing for once and make sure he is cared for before I can be really happy with Miles.

I'm not sure how long we cling to each other for but as soon as I can tell he is more relaxed, I say softly, "Listen, I'll go to Fleur's tonight on my own. It will be too much for you, being in Anton's house, seeing his girlfriend and hearing her talk about him. Stay here, but promise me you won't drink. I'll leave as soon as I can and we can talk some more."

James looks up and shakes his head. "It's fine. I'll come with you because quite honestly, I could do with a change of scene. It won't matter about being in Anton's house. It will be quite comforting really and if people do talk about him, I will welcome hearing it. I miss him so much, Miranda, and telling you has been cathartic. I needed that and perhaps it's something I should do with a counsellor. It's obvious I need to speak about my grief before I can move on. Don't put your plans on hold because of me. I'll be fine and as soon as this mess with the burglary is sorted, I'll go away and have a change of scene and, who knows, perhaps I'll find some happiness of my own."

The guilt threatens to choke me as I think about what I did. Anton's Rolex is safely in my pocket, so I can slip it back before anyone discovered it was missing. I have to go to Fleur's tonight for that reason alone and my heart breaks as the full enormity of what I've done hits me. I hate myself.

CHAPTER 4

VENETIA

"*H*oney, I'm home."

My heart starts beating madly as I prepare to tell Matthew something I can't take back when I've said it. I've decided to tell him I'm pregnant and pretend it's his. It may be, anyway, so it's only a half-lie and I tell myself this is for the best all round.

Fixing a smile on my face to hide how nervous I am, I go in search of him and, on seeing him, run into his arms.

"I missed you."

He hugs me tightly and says softly, "I missed you so much. I can't wait for Rome."

I snuggle into him and say in a muffled voice. "I have some news."

He pulls back and looks at me quizzically as I smile. "I'm not sure how you're going to take this, but I'm... we're - pregnant."

The look on his face causes me to break down because he cannot disguise the pure joy that breaks out across his face. He shouts, "Pregnant! Oh my god, we're going to have a baby, I can't believe it."

He lifts me up and laughs loudly and I giggle along with him and my heart settles. Yes, Matthew is my baby's father. I just know it. He has to be.

He puts me down and kisses me so passionately I melt against him. He strokes my hair and whispers, "Thank you."

"For what?"

"For making me the happiest man alive. I love you Venetia, so much it hurts."

The tears fall as I stutter, "I love you more. I don't deserve you and know you will make a fantastic father to our baby."

He wipes the tears away with his fingers and kisses each one of my eyelids before planting another toe curler on my lips, then he groans. "Must we go out tonight?"

Laughing, I drag him towards the kitchen where his supper is waiting and say firmly, "Yes, we do. We owe it to Fleur but don't worry, we have Rome where it will be just the three of us."

I laugh at the broad grin that breaks across his face as he places his hand on my stomach. "Our baby. How I love the sound of that."

Some moments in life are more treasured than most and this is one I want to wrap in that special place in my heart where the sweetest memories live and then revisit it forever. That special moment when life is perfect in every way and the future is bright and promising. This is our moment when everything comes right and I promise to spend my life making this wonderful man happy. It may have been a bumpy road getting here, but I made it and with the right man alongside me. I am quite emotional as I say with rare emotion, "I really love you, Matthew Stanmore."

His eyes soften and he pulls me close again and whispers against my lips, "I love you more, Mrs Stanmore."

As tempting as it is to forget about going to Fleur's party, I resign myself to getting ready and spending a few hours making polite conversation with my friends. Above all, I'm dreading seeing Anthony there and wonder how things will be between us. I'm also curious to see what Fleur's been doing while she's been away and long to hear more details of Miranda's trip to New York.

So just before eight o'clock, we head across the road and I couldn't be happier than walking with the man I love beside me. Some may call this the calm before the storm. Some storms you are warned are coming and some are unexpected, destructive and life-changing and to be honest, I should have done, but I never saw this one coming.

CHAPTER 5

FLEUR

"*A*re you nervous?"

Am I? A shiver passes through me as I think about the evening ahead. "I suppose I am a little, but in a good way."

Darren smiles and hands me a glass of wine and I smile my thanks. Yes, Darren has proven to be a good friend when I needed one the most and was the first person I turned to when the shock hit.

He looks around him and shakes his head. "I always knew you had a lovely home, but even I never appreciated just how magnificent this place is."

Looking around, I must agree with him. This house is magnificent, like the man who provided it. A lone tear escapes as I think about Anton. He must have been in Hell before he died. Darren walks over and says softly, "Hey, no more tears. He wouldn't want that, not tonight."

I smile through them and say with a break in my voice, "It's hard, though."

Darren takes my glass from my hand and pulls me close,

stroking my hair and whispering, "I've got your back. We'll do this together—for Anton."

I lean into him and marvel at how things have changed. Anton was always my rock, the man I loved and my best friend and now he's gone his place has been partially filled by an amazing man. Darren is just a friend, despite what my friends may believe when they see him. To be honest, I couldn't care less because the people that matter know already. They understand that he has helped me out with a problem that was way too big for me. He's been there to prop me up when I couldn't stand for grief and his family has helped me solve a mystery that hurts so much every time I think about it.

Pulling away, I say softly, "Thank you."

He shrugs and smiles sweetly. "I will always be here for you, babe. Don't worry about that."

As I look around, it settles my heart a little that I'm not doing this on my own. Who knows what will happen when I play my trump card, but until then, I must play the perfect hostess and make this an evening no one will ever forget?

As the soft music that Anton loved so much pipes through the house and the fire burns in the grate, creating a welcome atmosphere, I gaze around me with satisfaction. Yes, this is the perfect place to get justice for Anton. Now all I need are the players.

It doesn't take long before the doorbell rings and I take a deep breath and grin. "Here goes nothing."

Darren waits while I head towards the front door and wonder who will be first. As I open the door, I'm happy to see Arabella standing beside Anthony, although from the expression in her eye, something's happened. I wonder what he's done now. Anthony, on the other hand, looks as if he hasn't got a care in the world and smiles happily. "Fleur, darling, you are as gorgeous as always. The break must have done you good."

I smile politely and welcome them inside, taking pleasure in seeing the surprise on Anthony's face as he sees Darren behind me. "Oh, I don't think we've had the pleasure."

He holds out his hand and says loudly, "Anthony and you are?"

"Darren, a friend of Fleurs."

He turns to Arabella and winks. "Looking good, Bella."

Anthony stiffens at the familiar greeting, and Arabella laughs. "Hi Darren, it's good to see you."

She turns to Anthony and says with an impish grin. "Darren's a personal trainer at the country club as well as being Fleur's trainer. He's a great favourite with us all."

We all share a smile as Anthony looks a little put out and luckily the doorbell rings, removing me from the situation. I leave them to it and find Venetia and Matthew looking so happy it brings a tear to my eye. I don't miss that they are holding hands and notice that Venetia is looking the happiest I've seen her in years. Matthew says sweetly, "It's good to see you, Fleur. We've missed you."

I smile and kiss him on both cheeks before hugging Venetia and whispering, "You look amazing. What's your secret?"

She smiles and taps the side of her nose. "All in good time, honey."

As they follow me inside, I already know. It's obvious. The only thing that surprises me is that they're so happy about it. Matthew perhaps, but Venetia never struck me as the maternal type. I feel uneasy about what may happen and say a little too brightly, "Guys. Look who I've found."

I watch carefully and notice Anthony nod coolly and Arabella walks forward, smiling sweetly. "Venetia, how lovely you look and Matthew, I need to return your car first thing tomorrow morning."

He looks surprised. "You can keep it for as long as you like, you know that."

Anthony moves to stand beside his wife and smiles. "No need. Arabella's Porsche is being delivered home where it belongs."

We all stare at him in surprise as he says happily, "I have my old job back, and the future is looking amazing."

I watch everyone's reaction and although a little surprised, everybody congratulates him along with Arabella, who looks a little uncomfortable. While everyone is talking, I grab her arm and steer her into the kitchen. "What's going on?"

I'm surprised as the tears well up in her eyes as she says sadly, "Rather a lot as it happens. I can't talk now, but I'm not happy and could do with a friend to talk to."

We are interrupted by Anthony coming in search of his wife and he says in a whisper, "For god's sake, don't leave me with that couple. They could bore a man to death."

I peer at him in surprise, as does Arabella, and he shrugs. "What? I've never liked them."

Leaving them to it, I head to the door again as the final ring announces the last couple to arrive. As expected, Miranda stands there looking a little lost, and she says apologetically, "James will be along in a minute. He had to take a phone call as we were walking out of the door."

"That's ok. It doesn't matter. At least you're here. Let me get you a drink."

I don't think anything about Miranda hanging back a little as I head into the kitchen, but as I turn, I see her hurriedly removing her hand from the hall table. As she heads toward me, my eyes make out a gold object shining on the surface and the room spins. That wasn't there a moment ago and now it all makes sense. Anton's missing Rolex. I'd recognise it anywhere and when his parents reported it missing, I wondered where it could have gone. Now Miranda has unwittingly solved the riddle for me. Was it James or did she take? I'll probably never find out, but I'm glad it's back and I can return it to Anton's parents where it should be.

Taking a deep breath, I head into the room and my eyes search for Darren. He smiles reassuringly and I feel my lip tremble. Now they're here, I'm not sure I can go through with this, however, I can't until the final player arrives. I wonder where James is?

CHAPTER 6

FLEUR

*W*e make small talk for close on an hour before James arrives. When I answer the door, I can smell the alcohol on his breath and my heart sinks. Poor James. He looks at me nervously and I step forward and pull him close, whispering, "I'm sorry, James."

He pulls back and looks confused, and I shake my head sadly. "I just want you to know there are no hard feelings."

I'm shocked at the tears that well up in his eyes, and he nods. "Thank you."

I don't need to explain my comment because we both realise what I'm referring to. He's aware that I know and I'm telling him it's ok. I'm grateful when a comforting hand slips into mine and I see James's eyes widen as he sees Darren standing beside me. I introduce them and say softly, "Darren's been a good friend to me, James, and I hope you can forgive us for what we're about to do."

James looks confused and I beckon him to follow me to meet the others.

As they all glance up, I say with excitement. "James is

here, Darren get him a drink and then we can all move to the cinema room."

They all appear surprised and Arabella comes over and whispers, "What are you planning?"

I smile at her with what I hope is reassurance. "Putting things right."

There is nervous anticipation in the air as they all take a seat and I gaze around me at a room that was Anton's pride and joy. Glancing at my watch nervously, I notice Darren watching me and he nods and points to the door. My heart beats a little erratically and I know there's no going back. I make sure to dim the lights before he arrives and say loudly, "Ok, I've got a little surprise for you all. This may shock some of you and I'm sorry for that. However, Anton would want this to be shown, so here goes."

My heart thumps as I press 'play' and peer with interest at the surrounding faces, while trying hard to block out the sounds that turn my stomach every time I hear it. There is a shocked silence as the room is filled with an image of Anton and James. The one I took from his phone and the one he was being blackmailed over.

The tears pour down my cheeks as I witness the shock on everyone's faces mixed with disgust which tears my heart out. The video is graphic, pornographic and so x-rated it would be banned and I sigh as Miranda starts to sob and Venetia buried her face in her hands. Arabella starts to cry and James looks utterly destroyed. I am disgusted as I note interest in Anthony's eyes and can tell he is trying hard not to laugh. Matthew looks uncomfortable and has turned as white as a ghost.

After I think they've seen enough, I stop the video and turn the lights back on and notice Eddie had arrived. Eddie is Darren's brother and was the reason I went to stay with him in the first place.

As they all stare at me in horror, I say loudly, "May I introduce you all to Eddie Hodges?"

They all appear confused, and I share a smile with the brothers. "Eddie is Darren's brother and now a friend of mine. He has been instrumental in helping me solve the riddle of Anton's death and this video is the key."

Everyone looks shocked as Eddie nods. "Evening everyone."

I carry on. "Eddie is a detective in the metropolitan police. He was extremely interested in the information I gave him and has helped me through a difficult time."

I glance around to see who reacts to my news and just as I thought, one person in particular looks as sick as a dog.

I stand up and start pacing as I prepare to deliver a speech I have practised for days now and yet now it's come to it, it's a hard task to deliver.

Darren smiles his support and I take a deep breath. "As you all know, Anton died under mysterious circumstances. He was found by me, face down in our pool, fully clothed with many bruises on his face and body. What you don't know is that Anton was gay and in a relationship with James Donnelly."

There's a collective gasp around the room, and I smile at James. "I'm sorry about this, James, but I need to get this out in the open."

He nods and says with a quiver in his voice. "It's fine, carry on Fleur."

I turn and glance across at Eddie, who nods and I say seriously, "Anton was being blackmailed because of this video."

They all gasp and I carry on. "Both he and James received demands for large sums of money in return for the video not getting into the public domain. Anton was a celebrity and feared for his reputation as well as James's. They did everything they could to pay the money, but it was never enough. Anton became depressed as a result and James started drinking heavily. In desperation, Anton sought the services of a private investigator who managed to find the person responsible."

I steal a glance across the room and note that Darren and Eddie have moved to stand behind the person responsible and I steel myself. "He managed to trace the signal from the phone the blackmailer used and discovered it was very close. Extremely close, in fact, and came from just a few feet away."

The shocked faces stare around at each other as they realise what this means. It's one of us.

"So, as you have probably guessed, the blackmailer is actually sitting in this room. Isn't that right, Matthew?"

Everyone looks across at him in shock and Venetia cries out, "Matthew! You're wrong, of course, it wasn't him."

I laugh bitterly. "Are you sure about that, Venetia, because the expression on Matthew's face tells a different story."

Matthew shakes his head and Eddie says firmly, "There's no denying it because we checked out the files the investigator handed over. We also interviewed the receptionist at the hotel they used, who identified your picture as the man who stayed in the adjoining room. It appears that you got there early and managed to unlock the connecting door. You set up your phone to record the action and waited for the show to start. The cleaner remembers that you told her you wanted to leave a bottle of wine for your friends who were staying there and when she wasn't looking, you unlocked the door on their side."

James shouts, "We wondered who left the wine. Good God, Matthew, how could you?"

Matthew puts his head in his hands as Venetia cries out, "Matthew, tell them it isn't true."

He looks up at her and his eyes are blazing. "Yes, it's true, but I didn't kill Anton. I may have knocked him about a bit when he came steaming around, accusing me of all sorts, but he was no match for me and I let him have it. How was I to know he would kill himself rather than face the world knowing what he really was?"

I can't stand it and shout, "What he was! He was decent, caring, and an amazing man. I couldn't love him any more than I did, even though he betrayed me. How dare you speak about him as if he was nothing?"

I make to strike him, but one look from Eddie calms me down as Venetia sobs, "But why, Matthew, why do it?"

He looks across the room and his face contorts with rage as he snarls, "Because of him."

We all stare at the person he addressed his comment to, and Venetia turns pale as Anthony snarls, "Why me?"

Matthew starts to laugh. "Because you've been having an affair with my wife and I wanted it to stop."

Once again, the shock hits everyone in the room as Arabella cries, "No, this isn't true! Tell him, Venetia, not Anthony."

Anthony rolls his eyes and says wearily, "It is actually. Venetia and I had a fling for a bit, but now it's ended. I don't understand why Matthew did this; it doesn't make sense."

Venetia starts crying, as Arabella hisses, "You bitch, you were supposed to be my friend."

Venetia cries, "I still don't understand what this has to do with Anton and James."

Matthew snarls. "Because of you, Venetia. I was losing you because you were jealous of what they had."

He points to Arabella and Anthony and snarls, "You wanted to be her so badly. You wanted her house, her life, and her husband, and he was only too happy to oblige. I couldn't compete with that. We're not in their league, so I did what I had to do, and it worked."

She shakes her head and says sadly, "There never was a bonus, was there, Matthew?"

He slumps back in his seat. "No, the money I received from them is paying for the interior and our holiday. It worked though because as soon as you thought we had money; you came running back."

Venetia shouts, "That's not the reason why, and you know it! I came back because I couldn't stand him and I love you. I do love you, Matthew, and I can't believe you went to so much trouble for me."

Arabella shouts, "I can't believe what I'm hearing! You think Matthew blackmailing James and Anton is an act of love for you? I can't believe you would be so shallow and as for you..."

She turns to Anthony and says sadly, "You had an affair with one of my best friends and don't even seem to care. You pretended to have cancer so I wouldn't question you when I found your hotel receipt and you lied about losing your job because of a bloody programme you were planning. You're disgusting, Anthony and I don't recognise the same man I married."

Anthony looks at her and snarls, "You can't talk, can you darling?"

Arabella looks confused, and Anthony laughs bitterly. "Have you forgotten to tell me something?"

Arabella looks at him blankly and he laughs. "The day you were arrested, I came racing home as soon as Venetia called."

Arabella looks confused. "But you told me it was hours later, which is why you took so long."

His eyes flash as he throws her a look that would curdle milk. "I told you that because you believe anything I tell you. No, I found Venetia in your bathroom holding one of your pregnancy tests, my darling. A pregnancy test! You knew I didn't want children, and you decided that what I want didn't matter. You were going to have one regardless, and I can never forgive you for that."

Venetia starts to cry as Arabella says bitterly. "You talk about me lying when you're the master, it would seem. Anyway, so what if I do have a drawer full of pregnancy tests? You haven't been near me for so long they must be out of date by now? Not that it matters because I'm not pregnant, anyway."

She looks so sad my breath hitches and I long to run to her but Anthony laughs bitterly, "That's not what the test said my darling, even now you can't stop lying."

Arabella looks at him in disbelief and says in a broken voice, "I'm not pregnant, all of my tests have come back negative."

Now it's Anthony's turn to look as sick as a dog as he looks across the room at Venetia and says roughly, "It was yours, wasn't it?"

Arabella cried out as Venetia nods, the tears streaming down her face and Anthony yells, "You fucking bitch. You let me think it was Arabella's, and I was so angry we had sex in our bed while my wife was frightened and alone in a police cell. How could you?"

I'm guessing the whole room hates Venetia right now, and Arabella starts sobbing loudly as Venetia says in a broken voice, "I'm so sorry, Arabella."

Arabella starts to shake as I say icily, "Get out, Venetia. You are no longer welcome here and take your lover with you. I never want to see either of you again."

Anthony looks at Arabella with panic written all over his face and says urgently, "Come with me, darling, we'll talk this through and find a way out of this."

She shakes her head and says in a broken voice, "Just go, Anthony."

He looks around helplessly as the whole room stares at

him in disgust and then stands with no more words spoken and heads out of the room. Venetia looks utterly destroyed and breaks down before our eyes, and Miranda says a little kindlier than any of us would say, "Maybe you should follow him, Venetia."

Venetia looks at Matthew, who now resembles a statue, and says, "I'm so sorry, Matthew. I really do love you and chose you, not him. I just know this is our baby. It must be."

Arabella starts crying again and my heart goes out to her. Fate is so cruel as to tear her heart out with her husband's betrayal and then rub her nose in it with the knowledge her husband is having a baby with someone else. I'm fearful for her and wonder if she'll ever recover.

I watch as Venetia stands and says to Matthew, "Come with me."

He makes to stand, but Eddie puts a firm hand on his shoulder and says, "Not so fast. Matthew Stanmore, you are under arrest for blackmail, extortion, and manslaughter. You have the right to remain silent...."

As he reads Matthew his rights, the whole room remains silent as the shock hits each one of us and I sink to my knees as the tears fall thick and fast. It's over.

 Anton's death has been revenged and opened up a can of worms that has affected each and every person who lives here. Then I feel a strong hand pull me into an equally strong chest as Darren wraps his arms around me and gives me the comfort I need right now.

As Matthew follows Eddie out, James says loudly, "How did you know about us?"

Matthew turns and the whole room falls silent as he laughs bitterly. "It was by chance, really. I was following Venetia and as luck would have it, I saw you and Anton heading into the hotel. I didn't guess at first, but something sowed a seed of doubt in my mind and I kept a close eye on you both. It didn't take me long to realise what was going on, so I turned my attention to the two of you instead. I worked out that the only way to keep my wife was to get a lot of money to keep her happy and I knew the two of you were loaded. It wasn't personal, just a business decision."

I think his words shock everyone in the room as he reduces what he did to a business decision. It's so cold and unfeeling and I'm starting to believe that he and Venetia were a match made in heaven after all. I'm barely conscious of Eddie leading Matthew out, closely followed by Venetia, leaving Arabella, James and Miranda staring at one another in shock.

CHAPTER 7

FLEUR

*T*he next morning, the cold light of day is like the smoke from an extinguished fire. A raging inferno that has left ashes in its wake and the acrid smell of betrayal.

Miranda and James left soon after the others and Arabella stayed with me because she couldn't bear to go home. Darren also stayed, and the three of us are now staring at each other across the breakfast bar, as we struggle to understand what last night now means for all of us.

Darren must feel a little uncomfortable because he says with concern, "Listen, you probably want some time to talk. Perhaps I should head home for a bit."

I say quickly, "Please stay. Maybe just have a workout or go to work, but please stay."

I don't know why, but Darren has fast become someone I can't do without. Perhaps it's the comfort he brings me, or the fact he's not involved in any of the betrayals, unlike my so-called friends, but I've come to depend on him and can't bear the thought of him leaving me too.

He nods and smiles reassuringly. "I won't go anywhere,

don't worry. I'll head into the garden and have a workout and let you talk. You know where I am if you need me."

I breathe a sigh of relief and look at him gratefully and as the door closes behind him, Arabella says, "You like him, don't you?"

I stare at her in shock and she smiles. "It is ok to have feelings for somebody else, even if you love another. Surely you learned that last night."

She laughs at my expression. "Anton was in love with you and James, and the love he had for each of you was equal. He wouldn't want you to turn your back on happiness out of loyalty to him. I know that for sure."

The tears fall yet again as I stutter, "You know, Arabella, everybody always believed I was with Anton for his money. They saw me apparently living the high life at his expense, but it wasn't like that."

Arabella smiles, "I know."

"You were the only one then. The thing is because I loved Anton so much, it's as if I've lost my right arm. I suppose I never really realised how much I did love him until he died and now I'm struggling. However, there was always something between Darren and I. An invisible cord that bound us together and kept me anchored to him. I think even Anton saw it. Darren was the first person I turned to when it happened, and it wasn't just because of Eddie. I'm not sure why, but I need to be with him; does that sound cold?"

Arabella shakes her head sadly. "We can't choose who we fall in love with, or when. When you look around us, love has featured heavily in this mess and the lengths things people will go to for it. Take Matthew as a prime example. He was prepared to do anything to keep Venetia, and she was driven by wealth and greed. James was prepared to do anything for love, as was Anton, because they couldn't bear their secret coming out. We all love in different ways and now, in the cold light of day, I'm starting to realise that the person we need to love the most is ourselves. If we're happy, then the rest will follow.

I stare at her in sympathy and say gently, "So, what now? I'm sure you have some unfinished business across the road to take care of."

She nods and looks worried. "Yes, this won't be pretty, but I know what I need to do. Wish me luck, Fleur, because I am about to sweep out the trash in my life and start again."

I hug her tightly and say with feeling, "Good luck, Arabella. I'm here if you need me. I think we're the only two people in this whole mess who can hold our heads up high."

She nods sadly. "You can, but I was still trying for a baby against Anthony's wishes. I suppose he has the right to be angry about that."

Shaking my head, I fix her with my best frown. "You've done nothing wrong but want what most women do - a family. If anything, he's in the wrong for not seeing what was important. What are you going to do?"

Arabella pulls herself up and says in a strong voice, "Get on with the rest of my life—without him in it."

As I watch her walk away, I'm afraid for her. This is a difficult path she's chosen, and I'm not sure if she's strong enough against a man like him. However, I was telling the truth. I'm here for her and will see her through what is sure to be a turbulent time.

As I turn to clear away the breakfast things, I catch sight of the canvas I had made of Anton looking down at me and smile. "I love you, babe. Always have done and always will. You can rest in peace now because it's over."

I feel a lightness to my spirit that wasn't there before as he smiles out at me. Yes, I always loved Anton and I always will, even if I do find love. Arabella's right, there is more than one type of love and I owe it to myself to be happy. It won't dull the memories or feelings that I had for Anton. Those will never change, but I want to be happy—isn't that the dream, after all?

CHAPTER 8

MIRANDA

I'm still in shock over what happened last night. I was grateful that James had told me already because if I had seen that video without being forewarned about his affair with Anton, it would have destroyed me.

When I think of what Matthew and Venetia did, it makes my blood run cold. All night long I pictured Matthew in his prison cell awaiting trial and Venetia, alone and afraid at home. Maybe I should go and check on her, but I just can't bring myself to even look at her after what she did to poor Arabella.

Out of all my friends, Arabella is the only one who hasn't done anything wrong. She's kind, loyal and a fighter because she handled the whole bankruptcy thing with class and pride. Then, when she discovered about Anthony and Venetia's betrayal, she acted with dignity and I couldn't admire her any more than I do.

Sighing, I get up and think about poor James. Last night was devastating for him and we talked long into the night after we got home. In a funny sort of way, I think he had closure at Fleurs and despite the shock, seemed more positive than I've seen him in ages. Maybe he will be ok, I certainly hope so because I came to a decision last night, I am leaving today for New York.

Last night showed me that life is too precious to spend wasting it on things that don't make you happy. Miles makes me happy, so I am taking my original flight with James's blessing.

I begin to get ready, filled with excitement for a future that looks bright and promising.

It doesn't take me long and as I make myself breakfast, James appears and smiles ruefully. "You're leaving then."

I experience a pang as I stare at my husband and remember how happy we used to be and then nod and say softly, "I do love you, James, and care a great deal about what happens to you. If you want me to stay, I would, you know."

He crosses the room and pulls me close, whispering, "I know you do. However, you have a new life waiting and it will make me the happiest man alive to see you enjoying it. You deserve it, darling. It's all I ever wanted for you and I let you down in every way possible."

I stare at him and say angrily, "You never let me down. If anything, it was me who let you down."

"You?"

I nod miserably and sit down heavily. "I need to say something before I leave, and you're not going to like it."

James looks worried and I smile through the tears that have gathered as I think of how far I fell. As I confess all my sins to James about the jewellery, the pawnshop and the subsequent burglary, it's as if a weight has shifted from my heart. I almost can't look at him when I finish, but when I do, I'm surprised to see him smiling broadly. I'm in shock as he starts to laugh uncontrollably and I say in surprise, "What's so funny?"

He shakes his head. "I can't believe you did that; its pure

genius. I would have loved to see you dressed up as your friends and, to be honest, it now makes sense of a lot of things."

"Such as?"

"The clothes that appeared from what I thought was surely the best charity shop in the country. The excitement in your eyes when you wore them and the fact that you never asked me for money outside of what I gave you. I should have guessed you were up to something."

I say in shock. "Aren't you angry about the jewellery, I mean?"

"Not really. I never could stand that vulgar stuff my mother wore. Keeping it in the safe meant I didn't have to look at it and bring back the memory of a vain and shallow woman. You know, she was always putting me down and making me feel inadequate. She stifled me from a very early age and probably turned me off women forever."

He notices my face fall and reaches across the table and takes my hand in his. "I loved you though, Miranda. You were a little force of nature that crashed into my life one fine day as my new legal secretary. You brightened up a dusty office and brought the sunshine in. I fell in love with you almost immediately and longed to be at work just to see your beautiful face."

He wipes away my tears as he says gently, "I still do love that side of you, darling. What you just told me isn't that much of a surprise. You were always resourceful and only you would think of such an inventive way out of your problems. I'm impressed more than angry, so wipe away your tears and move on with my blessing."

The doorbell rings and I smile. "That's my cab. Now it's come to it, I don't want to leave. How ironic is that?"

James pulls me up and says firmly, "Go and make that new man of yours life hell instead of mine. Just make sure you keep in touch and keep me supplied with stories of what you get up to. Perhaps now we're no longer together, I can become your gay best friend and we will have a better relationship."

Impulsively, I hug him tightly and say tearfully, "I will miss you, and for the record, I love you with all my heart."

The doorbell rings again and I smile through my tears and say with excitement, "This is it, my new life."

James walks with me to the door and as I open it, I am shocked to see two police officers standing there instead of the taxi driver. My face falls as I say anxiously, "Can I help you?"

One of them steps forward and says firmly, "Miranda Donnelly?"

My heart starts racing as I say in a quivering voice, "Yes."

"You are under arrest for burglary, theft, breaking and entering, and fraud. You have the right to remain silent…"

I hear nothing else as I begin to shake and am grateful for James holding me up as he says angrily, "This is preposterous. You can't do this."

The other officer says, "I think you'll find we can. You may want to call a solicitor because your wife is going to need one."

They take my arms and I cry out in fear, "James!"

He follows us out saying, "It's ok, I'll call the office. We'll sort this, don't worry about that."

As I duck my head into the police car, I gaze around with fear. This can't be happening. I'm due to start again in New York. This is all wrong.

James's worried face stares after me as the car leaves The Chase and the tears fall freely. How did this happen? I am such a fool because now I have ruined everything.

CHAPTER 9

VENETIA

I didn't sleep a wink all night. I couldn't with everything playing on my mind. I can't believe it, Matthew - a blackmailer. I'm still in shock because he was the last person I thought would ever do this.

My heart goes out to James and Anton, and especially Anton. Matthew may not have killed him, but he had a hand in his death. It's so frightening to think of what the future now holds. Pregnant and alone, that's me and we'll probably lose the house because I've no doubt Matthew will go to prison and we will need the money to fight his case.

The pressure starts to build in my head and I sob as I remember the hatred directed at me and Anthony yesterday. They hate me—us and it's all my fault. How could I have started something with my friend's husband? Matthew was right when he said I wanted Arabella's life. It's been so hard living here as the poor relation, watching my friends enjoy a charmed existence and living the dream. I wanted that, who wouldn't and now my own selfish wishes caused everything to crash and burn.

I move to the window and gaze out across the cul-de-sac.

The curtains are still drawn all around The Chase and I wonder what happened when I left.

I notice a police car enter through the electric gates and wonder why we never had them repaired. Anyone can get in; they just drive up to it and they open. We were so sure nobody would ever trouble us we wouldn't pay to have the entry system repaired. Not that it matters because we would always let the police in anyway, but at least we would have had some warning.

My heart thumps as the car crawls along and fully expect it to stop outside my door. It must be connected to Matthew; it can be here for no other reason. However, it moves past and stops outside Miranda and James's house, and I stare as the uniformed officers make their way to the front door.

It doesn't take long before the door is opened and I watch in disbelief as they take Miranda off with them. I can tell she is crying and shouts out to James, who stands there looking shaken.

I pull back in case they notice me and wonder what's happening. Why have they taken Miranda? Maybe it's connected to the burglary and they need a statement. Yes, that's probably it.

I catch sight of Anthony's car in the driveway and my heart twists. He was so cold and callous last night and acted as if he had done nothing wrong. I'm not sure why that surprises me, because he's always been like that. He appears to have no shred of emotion inside him and I pity Arabella for having him as her husband.

As I turn away, it strikes me how ironic that is because I wanted to be Arabella so badly - they got that right. The trouble is, I am nothing like her because I'm fast realising that it's not the money or house a person owns that makes them admirable. It's the person they are inside and Arabella is one of the best.

As I wander downstairs, I glance around my own sparse home and feel angry. It's not fair. As far as I can make out, I am the one who has lost out in all this. I'm the one with a baby on the way and no father to help. I'm the one who will deal with the fallout from Matthew's jealousy, and I'm the one who will be hated more than anything by the women I once classed as friends.

Finding an inner strength to power me on, I wrench open the front door and march with determination towards Anthony and Arabella's home. He can jolly well pay for what he did, and I'm not going to let him get away with it.

I ring the doorbell continuously until I hear a terse, "Ok, I'm coming, you don't have to shatter my eardrums."

The door opens and Anthony stands there, looking at me in surprise. Then he laughs bitterly and looks me up and down and says derisively, "You're not at your best in the mornings, are you darling? It looks as if I had a lucky escape."

I follow him into his house and yell, "How dare you! How bloody dare you try to act as if this is nothing! You made this baby with me and now you're going to pay."

Anthony laughs and sneers, "You forget I never wanted a baby and just because you couldn't control your own contraception, you expect me to pay. Don't make me laugh. You're deluded, Venetia. A deluded fool because if you think I want anything more to do with you, you're deranged. Now, show yourself out and have a nice life."

I watch him head upstairs and as he starts whistling, I see red. Racing after him, I scream, "You bastard! I won't let you get away with this. You'll pay for this baby if I have to drag you through the courts. Then where will you be, the famous film producer with his name mud in the gutter press? Yes, I will draw this one out for years and make my money the easy way. In fact, it will be most satisfying dragging you down and watching you fall."

I grab hold of his arm as he reaches the landing, and he snarls, "Haven't you learned anything about blackmail from your husband? Look where it got him."

As the last word leaves his lips, we hear a voice say angrily, "I can't believe it. After everything that happened last night, you're still rubbing my face in it. What's the matter, Anthony? Couldn't you bear the thought of sleeping alone?"

We turn in shock and notice Arabella standing at the foot of the stairs with her eyes blazing. Anthony turns to me and shouts, "Look what you've done, you stupid bitch! You're poison, do you know that?"

He pushes me angrily and it happens so quickly I don't register what happens next, as my foot slips and I fall backwards. I experience a surge of pure terror as I tumble down their stairs, and the last thing I see is Anthony's shocked face watching me.

CHAPTER 10

ARABELLA

*S*omeone is screaming and they can't appear to stop and it's only when Anthony slaps me around the face that I realise it's me.

The tears run like rivers down my face as I stare at the crumpled body at the foot of the stairs. A pool of blood begins to form on the polished marble floor and I can tell she's dead. Her body is at an unnatural angle, and it appears that her neck is broken because her head is hanging limply beside her body.

Anthony cries out, "Stop screaming and think. Oh my God, you saw it, Arabella, she fell. It was an accident. Oh God, this is bad. Please tell me you saw that she fell."

I shake my head and say in a frightened voice, "We should call the police, ambulance, anyone, they could help."

Anthony appears to be in shock because he says quickly, "Remember what happened? She took a step back and fell. I tried to stop her from falling; tell them, Arabella, tell them it was an accident."

I'm not sure where it comes from, but I dial the emergency number as if a robot has replaced anything human inside me.

Calmly, I tell the operator what's happened and my address and then look at Anthony weeping on the floor like a child. I walk over to Venetia's lifeless body and gaze down on a woman who wrecked so many lives. Then my heart sinks as I notice another life ebbing away as a result of her foolish actions. The pool of blood is coming from between her legs and I cry for the life that is ending before it began. Anthony's baby. The one thing he never wanted and the one thing I wanted above everything else. Now it's gone and I cry as if it was my own. Huge wails echo around my perfect home, and I sink to my knees and cry for the only innocent person in all of this. It's only as we hear the sirens heading our way that Anthony appears to react to the situation and says in a hard voice, "I'll do whatever you want, give you everything you want, this house, the savings, everything, but back me up on this and say it was an accident. I can't go to prison, you know that. If I go down, you go down with me. We need to stick together."

Suddenly, the place is full of activity and I stand aside and watch Anthony taking charge. I watch the police cordon off the area around Venetia's body, and men in white overalls invade my house. I am taken into the living room where a police officer asks me questions, but I don't hear him. All I can think of is what Anthony said. Is this really how it ends? We walk away from this whole mess as the only ones untouched by tragedy. We get to move on with our lives and watch everyone else dealing with the fallout. Can we really keep the dream intact and move on to a bright future? As I sit like a statue, those and a thousand other thoughts crowd around my mind and then I hear her voice, Desdemona Fortune. 'Beware the Ten Commandments'.

I never really knew what she meant by that, but now it's

painfully clear. We have broken every single one of them between us in one way or another. The final one is up to me before the circle is complete. 'You must not bear false witness against your neighbour.'

Can I really lie to get Anthony in the clear at the cost of justice for Venetia? If I do, I would be the same as all of them. I would be part of that elite club that protects itself and moves on. It's not as if it will make any difference to her, anyway. After all, her life will not go on. No, surely, it's not that big a deal in the grand scheme of things. It would be so easy to tell a white lie because I did see Anthony push her out of the way. It was an accident and certainly not deliberate, but should I do that for him? Then I wonder what she really meant that day. Perhaps it was a warning that if you go against the Ten Commandments, your life will be destroyed. I've already broken one of them by not respecting my parents. Can I really add false witness to my sins?

The officer clears his throat and says kindly, "I'm sorry, madam, I know you're in shock, but I really need to hear your account of what happened."

As I gaze up, I see him looking at me with concern with his pen and pocket notebook at the ready and I say firmly, "It was Anthony. He pushed her."

EPILOGUE

ARABELLA

ONE YEAR LATER

"Who do you think they are?"

Fleur whispers, "I don't know, but there are loads of vans. They certainly have a lot of stuff."

We watch from our vantage point from the spare room window and I say thoughtfully, "The house sold quickly enough. That's good."

She nods. "Yes, despite the publicity, they don't appear to have been put off."

We watch as a woman drives into The Chase in a large Range Rover, closely followed by a man in a Ferrari. Our eyes widen as the car door slams and a slim, elegant woman jumps out.

Fleur says, "How old do you think she is?"

"It's hard to tell, early thirties maybe."

We look as the man races over to her and lifts her into his arms and carries her squealing towards the house. Fleur laughs softly, "He's not, though. How old would you say he is?"

"Early fifties perhaps."

We turn to each other and grin. "Interesting."

We both say the word at the same time and then dissolve into laughter.

We make our way downstairs for the usual coffee and I say thoughtfully, "I still can't believe we have new neighbours."

Fleur nods. "I suppose Matthew needed the money to pay his solicitor. Not that it did him any good. Ten years for blackmail was a little excessive."

I nod. "Yes, but it caused a man to take his own life. I'm sure he'll be out earlier for good behaviour, which is a lot sooner than Anthony."

Fleur looks at me with concern and I shrug. "He deserved every year they gave him. I know him though and he'll work it, so he gets an open prison and the life of Riley. He'll be out sooner than we think, but he won't be coming home here."

We grin at each other as Fleur says, "I can't believe he agreed to the divorce after your damning testimony against him. He never even fought it and in effect signed away all his rights to the house, cars, and savings. I was impressed because for the first time, he did something noble."

"Yes, but you've got to understand he had an ulterior motive for doing so."

"Which was?"

"He gets to keep all his future earnings and by the sounds of things, his new project is set to earn millions. Don't be fooled by Anthony's generosity, Fleur, there is only one person he cares about – himself."

I stare at my friend and smile. "Talking of caring. How is the delectable Darren?"

Laughing, Fleur hugs herself and says happily, "Every bit as amazing as I always thought he would be. His new gym is doing well, and he's got twenty people working for him now."

"Do you worry about him? I mean, he's super fit and we both know what a woman magnet he is?"

She shrugs, "I can't worry about that because if it happened, it just means it wasn't meant to be. I'm not losing my trust in someone based on another's infidelity."

She laughs. "Now it's your time to spill. I heard Eddie has moved in. You kept that one quiet."

She links her arm in mine and says happily, "Who knows, we could end up as sisters, after all. What do you say to a double wedding?"

Laughing, I shake my head as Eddie heads into the room. "What wedding?"

We dissolve into fits of laughter and he rolls his eyes. "I'll never understand women."

Moving across, I kiss him gently on the cheek and marvel at how I found this amazing man. Like his brother, he is totally gorgeous to look at with rugged good looks and an amazing body. His eyes twinkle and many women would kill for those long, dark lashes and he treats me like a princess.

He wraps his arm around my waist and says gently, "I've got to work but should be back by seven. How about I take you to that new bistro that's just opened in town?"

He looks across at Fleur and says brightly, "You too, Fleur. Bring that brother of mine and we can make a night of it."

Fleur grins. "Consider it a double date."

He laughs and as I watch him head off to work, I feel a happiness I always wanted but never really got. Eddie completes my perfect world because he is genuine. He loves me unconditionally and I trust him with my life. I still work at the country club, although I am in the process of setting up my own Interior design company. I already have two clients with huge budgets, so the future is looking good.

Fleur says, "Have you got any of those flyers you had printed? Perhaps you should drop one into the new neighbours. Your home is all the advertising you need and we could find out everything about them over a coffee."

The doorbell rings before I can answer her and I'm happy to see Miranda standing there when I open the door. She grins in her impish way and says, "Have you seen the cars across the road? I'm guessing an actor or something along those lines."

She follows me inside and says brightly, "We need to celebrate, ladies. I've now completed my final hour of community service and officially a free woman."

We rush to congratulate her and she breathes a sigh of relief. "Thank God that's over. Now I can start again."

I stare at her with interest. "What will that involve?"

"Well, James has told me that he's moving in with his boyfriend. Apparently, he has a flat in Westminster, not too shabby either by the sounds of it, so I'm getting a lodger to help pay the bills. James said he would still pay the mortgage until I find my feet and I have my job at the solicitors to keep me in shoes, but I'll need help in selecting the most suitable applicant."

Fleur laughs. "You mean the fittest, most wealthy, applicant."

She laughs and heads back the way she came. "Just a flying visit, ladies, because I must draft my ad."

Fleur calls after her, "It won't be the first ad you've drafted. How are things going with the Internet dating?"

Miranda's laughter is all the answer we get and Fleur

grins. "It's a shame Miles gave up on her. Mind you, it was doubtful she would ever get accepted into the US with a criminal record, anyway."

I nod. "It is a shame because it sounds as if she had it all worked out and was set for life."

As I walk Fleur to the door, I feel a sudden rush of affection for my friend and say warmly, "You know, next time you have any bright ideas about visiting fortune tellers, can you count me out?"

She laughs. "I could say the same to you, although I did hear about a medium…."

I quickly push her out of the door and slam it shut, and I hear her laughter float across the path as she heads home. Yes, despite our first impressions, Desdemona Fortune was spot on. My friends did hold the key to my destiny and luckily for me, I escaped more lightly than they did.

Another knock on the door, brings me back to the present and laughing, I open it saying, "Ok what did you forget…"

I stop as I see the stunning woman from across the road standing there, looking at me with a huge smile on her face. "I hope you don't mind me bothering you, but I'm new as of today and wanted to introduce myself. My name's Ava and my husband is called Sebastian. We are so keen to get to know the neighbours and wondered if you would like to join us for social drinks this evening?"

I smile warmly. "That would be lovely. I'm Arabella, and my partner is Eddie."

She smiles and looks around with interest, saying, "You know, this place seems so quiet. It's what we loved about it. Big gates to shut the whole world out and live a quiet and relaxing life."

I nod. "Yes, it's certainly a special place, that's for sure."

She smiles and says brightly, "I'll see you later. I'm off to introduce myself to the others. Are they nice?"

I nod. "The best. You'll be very happy here."

As I close the door, I laugh to myself. Yes, Ava and Sebastian will fit in perfectly.

~

If you enjoyed this story you may be interested in The Summerhouse Girls

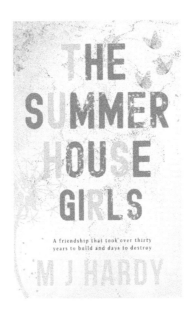

Thank you for reading Living The Dream.
If you have enjoyed the story, I would be so grateful if you could post a review. It really helps other readers when deciding what to read and means everything to the Author who wrote it.
NB: This book is written in UK English

. . .

Connect with me on Facebook

Check out my website

Thank you

BEFORE YOU GO

Thank you for reading.
If you have enjoyed the story, I would be so grateful if you could
post a review. It really helps other readers when deciding what to
read and means everything to the Author who wrote it.

Connect with me on Facebook

Check out my website

Thank you

I feel very fortunate that my stories continue to delight my readers. I couldn't do it without your support, and I thank every one of you who has supported me.

For those of you who don't know, I also write under another name. S J Crabb.

You will find my books at sjcrabb.com where they all live side by side.

As an Independent Author I take huge pride in my business and if anything, it shows what one individual can achieve if they work hard enough.

I will continue to write stories that I hope you will enjoy, so make sure to sign up to my newsletter, or like my Facebook page, so you are informed of any new releases.

With lots of love and thanks.

Sharon xx (M J Hardy)

Ps: M J Hardy is a mash up of my grandmother's names. Mary Jane Crockett & Vera Hardy. I miss you both so much & wish you knew this chapter in my life. One of my fondest memories is sitting in my grandmother's rocking chair by her gas fire, reading her collection of Mills & Boon books when I was about 12 years old. I wonder what she thought of that – I dread to think!

CHECK OUT MY OTHER BOOKS

The Girl on Gander Green Lane
  The Husband Thief
  Living the Dream
  The Woman who Destroyed Christmas
  The Grey Woman
  Behind the Pretty Pink Door
  The Resort
  Private Island
  The Summerhouse Girls

You're Invited!

Join my Newsletter
Follow me on Facebook